Jake

An Extraordinary Tale of an Ordinary Dog

Jake

An Extraordinary Tale of an Ordinary Dog

Daniel Reiner

PRESS

Published by Vulpine Press in the United Kingdom in 2022

ISBN: 978-1-83919-476-4

www.vulpine-press.com

For the Millvale Writers Group. Their gentle nudges helped me to transform Jake from a single scene into the novel you hold in your hands.

Also by Daniel Reiner:

The Shadow Beyond

The Shadow Effect

It all began on a Friday afternoon at the park...

The Park!

In Jake's world, it was his favorite place of all—even more so than his own yard. Down the street, only minutes away, he could be there as many as three times per day in warmer weather. Off the leash, he would take advantage of releasing the pent-up energy of youth: playing with friends, running after balls, chewing sticks, chasing squirrels. So much to do! And, capping off each visit: a pass along the path through the trees that bordered the big, open field. The smells rarely varied much, but it was worth keeping track of who had been around.

This time, however, something was different.

Off the trail, a splash of yellow was tucked in amongst the weeds, a spot of brightness within the greenery.

Bird was his first thought, and correct. But it was toppled over, unmoving, legs stiff.

Dead.

Seeing it, the average person might identify the poor thing as a goldfinch. A smarter person, or at least one interested in ornithology, could take it a step further: *Spinus tristis*, and clearly a male due to the coloration.

But, as a dog, Jake ever leaned toward the pragmatic. For him, it was simply a dead bird, probably edible. He'd never eaten one, but knew that he could if he wanted to. Or, he felt that he could. It was a grey area. The food at home was always tasty, and the memory of *breakfast* made his mouth water. The next dependable meal was far off though, governed by an evening rhythm named *dinner*, and the bird was right here.

Tempted, his stomach rumbled. The feathers would be dry, but he could choke it down, then get a drink from the water fountain...

No.

Something about this particular dead bird was off-putting.

Jake knew death. There were clean deaths and messy deaths. This was a clean one, the body intact, but...bad. It wasn't the bad of rot and decay that causes sickness. That odor was easy to pick out. Here, all he sensed was standard death. This one was good to eat.

But, somehow, not good.

Despite knowing that dead things make no noise, he forced himself to be still anyway, canine faculties focused.

There was nothing to hear.

Taste?

Coming in close, he opened his mouth.

No!

He backed off. Without so much as a lick, he felt an aura of wrongness, unseen but nearly palpable. Intuition made it plain that the smallest touch would be a mistake.

Bad!

But bad how? To be sure, the thing could be pointed at. There was that, at least. But what about it, exactly? Sniffing from a safe distance didn't shed any light on the matter, and neither did views from different angles. It continued to both look and smell like a recently dead bird.

He pondered the situation intently.

And pondered.

And, at length, came to wonder: was the dead bird the badness itself, or was there some sort of dirt or residue on it? Something that could be washed off by the rain that seemed to be ready to fall.

He latched onto that, the notion of lingering odor deeply ingrained. He could be satisfied to believe that the badness was a smell—except for the fact that he'd already decided that it wasn't. If there was one thing he could trust, it was his nose. The feeling he had, barely quantifiable, was something else.

And so, he stared at it.

And stared.

And came to realize, on a subliminal—but indisputable—level, that it *wasn't* dead.

Alive?

He wouldn't—couldn't—go that far. The effort of trying to resolve the paradox of simultaneously being dead and not-dead dug furrows in his brow. A sudden dread of the unknown tightened his gut. His tail fell and curled between his legs.

A small whine escaped.

He considered a bark, but growled instead, using the sound reserved for those instances when truly vexed.

And as he growled, another thought arrived.

Not bird?

Could something look like a dead bird, smell like a dead bird, but not be a dead bird? Like a ball too big to fit into his mouth, the concept was too much to grasp. As far as small creatures went, there were birds and mice and snakes. What else? Fish were floppy and slippery, but still comprehensible. Bugs were crunchy and weird, but also still okay.

This dead-not-dead bird was something different. But how do you describe a quality that can be seen and yet not seen, smelled and yet not smelled?

Drops of rain began to spatter the ground.

"Jake!"

SHE was calling. He had to leave. The puzzle of the bird-thing would have to wait. But first, he would lay claim to it.

His bladder now empty, he ran to the comforting voice of his pack leader.

The following morning was Saturday, a day of extra sleeping. At least, SHE did. Jake always woke up at the same time for a trip through the little door out to the yard, followed by a drink. After that, it was a matter of waiting, as patiently as he could, for breakfast. That delay was the one thing he didn't like about Saturdays. Or Sundays, either. But, on the other paw, he would probably be going to the park earlier than on the other days.

That pattern held up. It was quite early when he arrived, and no other dogs were there yet. When SHE sat down on a bench, Jake headed off to check on the strange thing from the day before.

Gone?

Less than a day after finding it, the dead-not-dead bird-thing was gone. He knew precisely where it had been. His mark, that aroma of selfness, clung to the plants *there*. But the thing itself was nowhere to be seen or smelled. Other dogs had left their calling cards along the trail in the meantime, but none close to his. The nearest points of interest were a sapling and a large rock, both a long leap away. If his possession had been taken, canine-courtesy required that proof of new ownership be established.

But...

His forehead wrinkled as he realized that no other dog had even visited this patch. There wasn't the smallest whiff of fur-scent other than his own. Repeated circles around the area continued to yield nothing.

None?

No other animals had been through here—none at all. But, more remarkably, that small spot where the bird-thing had been, was scentless: a place of no-smell. The very idea was absurd! Everything had a smell: dogs, birds, people, balls. As perplexing as that was, the indefinable danger Jake had previously sensed was also gone. That made him feel a little better, a little bolder.

So, he sniffed again, more closely. And *something* registered.

Like all aspects of this bird-thing, it was mysterious: a wispy odor, there, then not, then back again: a *tickle* in the back of his nose. Or, an impression in his brain. And when there, it was not the least bit reminiscent of bird.

Intrigued, he jammed his snout straight down.

Yikes!

Jerking back, he couldn't contain a yelp, then a pair of angry barks. There was no pain, but the sensation was completely novel: his nose had gone numb. Similar things had happened to him before, but always with a leg or foot, never the nose. He scrunched it up, pawed at it a few times, and took a deep breath. Odors were still registering, thankfully. And yes—sensation was returning.

His exclamations hadn't gone unnoticed. Three familiar yips and the rapid-fire pace of short-legged running caught his attention. He didn't have to see the lightly colored fur to know who was coming.

Sandy.

He cantered over to meet his friend, and after exchanging greetings he tried to lead her back to where he'd been. She came part of the way, then stopped.

Between the two, Sandy was older, but not by much. Jake was more energetic and adventurous, so she deferred to him. She had always followed him—until now. Her stubbornness was more mystifying than insulting, and Jake had to understand why. Through subtle expressions, body and tail positioning, and a few growls, they talked over the situation.

"My bird-thing was there," explained Jake. "It's gone now."

"I can see that," responded Sandy.

"What's wrong?"

"It's bad."

Jake recalled his disquieting encounter from the day before, then the consternation and confusion from moments ago.

"Maybe," he allowed.

"Maybe? Use your nose! You're the only one who's been there."

"I'm the only one who's curious?"

"Curious? More like stupid!"

That was too much for Jake. He wasn't the brightest dog, but knew the difference between a squirrel and a chipmunk. Animated discussion ensued, civility regrettably lacking.

With Jake weighing about fifty pounds and Sandy a fifth of that, their throats produced vastly different frequencies. The complex, overlapping waveforms of their barks were magnified in some places, diminished in others. Harder objects caused a multitude of echoes, while softer surfaces took the edge off the harshest notes. In all of history, had such a combination of sounds ever occurred?

Perhaps.

But this time…

This time, it wasn't merely so much random noise to fade off into the distance. This time, the difference was their proximity to a tear in the fabric of space, the crack through which Jake's dead-not-dead bird-thing had squeezed the day before.

The crack that had almost sealed shut.

Almost.

The peculiar formula of their outburst reverberated across the multi-dimensional angles between worlds. Vibrations reflected and deflected among arcane and unseen facets. Amplified, an unfortunate energy accumulated. Unable to be contained, it spilled through, eroding the tenuous framework that underlies our universe.

The crack widened.

Reality *quivered*.

To be sure, it was subtle. Among people, only the most sensitive would have had a chance of picking up on it. But Jake felt it, and Sandy seemed to, as well. Both went still and concentrated on the world around them, looking and listening and smelling. But the fleeting nature of the event didn't allow any chance to zero in on it.

Though baffled, Jake was glad of the distraction. Sandy was his best friend. Between friends, disagreements should be voiced, then forgotten.

He took a final peek at the spot where the bird-thing had been. Curiosity was pushing him to investigate, but Sandy's friendship was more important. Another argument, so soon, would be bad. It was time to run and play, so they did.

Meanwhile, across the black gulfs of the endless void, an abominable alien horror observed from the other side of that crack. And learned.

***

Jake is running…

It's night, but fiercely hot, far worse than any summer day. He's zigzagging his way through a dense growth of trees, moving so swiftly that it seems his paws don't even touch the ground. A sickly moon glows with a bizarre, red-tinted light that casts unsettling shadows of leafless, skeletal branches. The air is thick with a pungent stench that sears his nostrils. And his heart is hammering, near bursting, but not only because of the heat and exertion.

There's fear, too.

Something is chasing him. Or maybe somethings. His vision had blurred when he snatched a glance back. Did he see one or two? Or more? He's not sure. The one thing he is sure about is that it is on his tail. He can imagine a hand or paw reaching out, trying to grab him, but he can't chance another look. The priority now is to go as quick as he can, put some distance between himself and whatever is back there. And with so many obstacles, it's not possible to go in a straight line. He swerves: left, right, left—

What?

The trees are moving! Not getting blown by the wind, the trunks themselves are shifting, trying to block him. He sees madness in trying to comprehend it, so doesn't. Repeatedly dodging and backtracking, progress is slow. Not far ahead is the edge of the woods. Beyond, a grass-covered clearing drops off downhill. Determined, he launches himself at it.

Yes!

Past the last tree, another leap puts him onto the slope. But it's immediately evident that something is very wrong.

Up?

Jake's eyes tell him that the ground slopes down—it does—but every bound is an effort, as if he is going up. As he slows, he feels the thing getting closer to his tail, that hand inches away…

Back!

With a burst of inspiration, he realizes that he can use the up-side-down landscape to his advantage. He locks his legs stiff, claws digging in. The strategy will be a standard one: If the thing is small enough, attack; if too large, dart between the legs and take off. Sliding to a stop, he whips around at neck-snapping speed and sees—

Nothing!

There's nothing there—nothing to either bite at or run under. But he can't let himself relax. Assisted by the oddly reversed gravity, he tears uphill faster than he could ever have imagined. Once back on the level, a turn right puts him on a course parallel to that sinister forest. He keeps a cautious eye out for any movement.

Before long, the feeling of a threat has dissipated, so he slows to a trot and catches his breath. No longer panicked, the scenery of the park is easy to identify, even in the darkness. And that foul odor is gone. And it's much cooler, much more like a regular summer night. And Sandy is over there, by the fence. She has to be warned!

Wait.

He has a hard time understanding what had happened: moving trees, an upside-down hill, an invisible pursuer?! How can he explain all of that to her? Their squabble from earlier fresh in his mind, Jake thinks it may be better to skip it and instead find a good stick for a game of tug.

In the pale light he spots a fallen branch underneath a tree. Suspicious, he approaches slowly…

Good.

The tree is behaving like it should, staying put. But the stick reveals its true nature as he nears, flexing and wriggling. It must be a snake, but none he's ever seen before: long and thin and black.

The thing strikes, wrapping tightly around his left front paw. With a growl, he bites at it, but the instant his teeth sink in, his whole snout goes numb. Startled, being pulled off balance, he falls. Another snake wraps around his body and holds him down. The loop tightens. He can't breathe! Then a third—

NO!

***

Awake, trembling, the familiar scents of home were reassuring, but only to a point. Jake listened until he was sure that SHE was breathing steadily.

Asleep.

If he had barked or whined, it must not have been very loud. The snakes had seemed so real! He tried to forget the dream and relax, but something nagged at him as being wrong in some vague

12

way. His eyes shot everywhere, including up, into the realm of birds. Obviously, there were no birds in the sleeping room. But there was nothing else either. There couldn't be. At night, inside, there was just the tiny pack: Jake and SHE.

Safe?

In the bed above him, SHE stirred, mumbled something, then was quiet again.

As the distress induced by Jake's nightmare faded, that weirdness continued to echo. He dozed in those hours before dawn, but not restfully. Each short episode was interrupted with a spasm of his real legs to flee a dream worry. But when enough of the rising sun leaked in around the curtains to show that the room held nothing out of the ordinary all the way up to the ceiling, he let himself relax a little.

Some muted chirps sounded, right outside the window. Befuddled by the dream imagery that remained and a memory of the more real, dead-not-dead bird-thing, Jake had to wonder about the source. But he knew what made those sounds to be small, brown, and innocuous. He relaxed further.

A singular odor stood out among the blurs, so he inhaled deeply, trying to sniff out anything bad...

Nothing.

One thing was different, though. The air was stuffy, as if pregnant with the rain of a storm. But, at this time of year, with the humidity of late summer outside in the yard and the park, there didn't seem to be a need to fret about that either. Everything was fine.

Thirsty.

The water was downstairs. As he left the room, the sight of the top step brought back a snippet of the dream strangeness. Was down actually down? Or would he have to fight his way to the bottom?

He eased forward, anxious. His right paw hovered in the air experimentally, trying to feel the tug of gravity.

Good.

Down was indeed down. Truly, everything was fine.

His thirst sated, Jake decided to head outside and check over the grounds. Though pleasantly cool, the heaviness of the air seemed to be the same as it had been in the house. The light of the sun was blocked by the leaves of the—

Trees!

Something about trees…and…leafless branches…swirled into his thoughts. But the associated fear failed to get a clawhold, fell apart, and blew away. For the most part. Not certain if all was fine or not, he forced himself to swallow his uneasiness.

At the edge of the porch, he had to stop when he caught sight of something that was both very normal and extremely abnormal.

Sandy?

Was it Sandy? A short way from the porch, but too far to scent, it sure resembled her. But this early? And she was standing so stiffly. Only her eyes moved, a tiny bit at a time: left, right, up, down. Suddenly, they stopped their wandering and locked onto something to his right. Jake glanced over and was stunned to see that SHE was here, beside him—and had managed to get there without making any noise at all. SHE was never that quiet. At the very least the big door always creaked loudly whenever it moved.

Sandy, also unnaturally silent to that point, was silent no more. She began to growl, her tiny eyes overflowing with hatred.

Why?

SHE had always been very nice to Sandy, often giving treats. Or throwing the red ball. Or giving a belly rub. And Sandy had always reciprocated with wags and licks. How could she have forgotten all of that?

But when SHE touched Jake, his world went crazy. An electric shock ripped through his body, forcing a tremble. Barely, he held his bladder. The images came next, a flood of loathsome things overlaying all that he saw. They had shapes he couldn't fathom, inside-out, upside-down. They spoke words that he knew he shouldn't know. Yet, he did. Their suggestions were nauseating.

But he refused to listen. He refused to be swayed into doing things he could never do.

And as he resisted, he became more aware of Sandy's terrible yipping and yapping, the same thing repeated over and over. Whatever the nonsense was, its shrillness hurt his ears, then his head. He grew dizzy, but even as the pain built, those pictures in his head, and their voices, faded.

Then SHE jerked away violently, breaking contact with Jake.

Though much of the fuzziness cleared, the air had become more stifling. He had to struggle to breathe.

Now, SHE was crying out in an agony that sounded far worse than how he felt.

Jake was convinced that Sandy was the cause of their pain.

STOP!

He let loose with warning barks, torn between drives of protection and friendship, but Sandy continued with her caterwauling. Then a frightful shriek behind him forced his paw: SHE had collapsed and was flailing around and screeching in a way he didn't think possible. He dove off the porch at Sandy, teeth bared for the attack. But, still dizzy, he lost his footing and fell in a heap.

As Jake strained to right himself, that oppressive feeling in the air vanished. The pain receding, his head unclogged.

Finally on his feet, he turned around.

SHE was gone.

"What did you do?" he barked at Sandy fiercely. "Where is SHE?"

"That wasn't SHE!" insisted Sandy. "It was a bad thing! See! The big door is closed!"

He looked back.

Closed!

Jake's mind boggled, but he handled the situation with typical canine aplomb: He dismissed it.

"What were you saying?" he asked more calmly.

"The chant of Not-Real. I banished it to—"

"You what?"

"Sent away. I sent it away, to—"

Behind them, the big door creaked loudly and swung open. SHE stepped out onto the porch.

"Sandy! Please! It's too soon for all this noise. Go home."

SHE pointed up the street.

Sandy obediently turned and headed off, but after slipping through a gap between fence and gate, she stopped. "The park," she yipped. "The usual time. And leave the dead birds alone!"

"Again," yapped Sandy.

Jake had been trying to learn the chant of Not-Real for some time now, his throat raw from the effort. It wasn't long, but the sounds were difficult to make. And on his best attempts a disturbing echo clattered between his ears, lessening the incentive to get it right.

"Gr'hm ngk'loh kh'rawr...k—"

"No hesitation! Speak it confidently. Again."

Jake swallowed, preparing for another try, but spied movement off to his left.

"Cat," he growled, heart pumping faster.

Sandy inspected the blob of grey fur crouched under a bush.

"Oh, that one," she huffed. "Ignore it."

Once he picked out the distinctive splash of white on its chest, Jake did recognize the cat as being from the neighborhood. And as being harmless. He wanted to look away, but the cat's eyes were so...interesting. As they locked gazes, it meowed in a way that was...soothing. But that didn't seem right. When had any cat ever been soothing?

Then it crept out a few paces and meowed again.

Though Jake had never thought of cats as friendly, he became convinced that this one was. And...trustworthy? Maybe. Regardless, there was nothing to get excited about. Nothing at all.

His heart slowed.

He yawned.

Wasn't it about time for a break? He was about to ask Sandy about that when he noticed her head dip.

The grey cat uttered its wonderfully relaxing sound a third time.

As he lay down, he saw Sandy do the same.

His eyelids drooped. And shut.

***

It's foggy. Very foggy. The area is illuminated by a dim, diffuse light from all around. Jake has no idea how he got there, but Sandy soon appears and stands next to him. Then another shape materializes from out of the whiteness…

The cat.

It stares at the pair for a moment, then slinks into the swirling mist. Curiosity causes them to follow, relying on noses and whiskers to find the way.

The cat-scent leads them to a stone wall, specifically to a hole in its base. Sandy is small enough to fit, but the overpowering odor of cat within rules that out.

Further exploration reveals another break in the wall: a doorway, but not a full-height one like the type a person might use. This entrance is sized for a dog. Through it, a path leads down into darkness. In spite of that unknown, and in contrast to the previous opening, this one smells…inviting. The odor reminds Jake of the park.

The pair could walk side-by-side, but only because Sandy is so small. It seems to be intended to be used single file, so Jake leads them down a ramp that bends to the right. Beneath their paws, the stone has enough texture to prevent any slips as they circle round and round, down and down.

At the bottom they emerge into a natural cavern, the high ceiling barely visible. Here, the stone floor is very smooth. And there's more light, the source obvious: Far away at the other end, flames burn tall and thin, looking more than anything else like a tree trunk on fire. Much closer by, the grey cat is sitting next to a man wearing a dark robe and a curiously tall hat.

As Jake and Sandy approach, the cat raises a paw, pointing at them.

"It was these two," he says to the man.

And Jake understands the words! Or sounds. Or whatever. All he knows for sure is that it wasn't a meow or purr. He's about to ask Sandy what's happening when the man speaks.

"You mentioned that the consensus among your kind is that the entity is Shabh-lith?" he asks the cat. Again, Jake grasps the words.

"Though the signs hint at that one, it cannot be. The uninformed jump to conclusions. The histories are very explicit about its fate."

"One of its kin, perhaps?"

"Very likely."

"Their kind know nothing of this world," says the man. "Is it wise to involve them?"

"It is necessary," shrugs the cat. "Things of this nature can often camouflage themselves, hiding better than any rat. The ultimate battle will be difficult, but we know that we can defeat it—if we can find it. We believe that Jake, the larger one, is attuned to it. The smaller one, Sandy, seems to have a great store of useful knowledge."

"They do not have a say in the matter?"

"No."

The man frowns slightly. "You'll guide them?" he asks.

"They will be guided."

"Very well."

The man turns to Jake and Sandy.

"My name is Kaman-Thah," he says, bowing. "I am one of the caretakers of this place. This is your first visit here. There is much for you to learn. I will try to answer any questions that you may have, but Algernon should handle the bulk of that. We shall see each other again."

And he bows again, then walks away, toward the fire at the far end.

"I am Algernon," the cat says to Sandy. "I heard and watched you trying to teach him. You are blessed with more patience than I gave you credit for. And I must admit that your skills are admirable. Clearly, it was you who did it. Do you know exactly what you did?"

"I banished an entity from beyond using the chant of Not-Real," replies Sandy. "It worked."

"Oh, it surely did."

"I saved our neighborhood. You live there, too!"

"I do. And you should know that your action saved more than the neighborhood. But consider this." He taps his paw on the floor twice. "As you, along with all other dogs, have been unaware of the true nature of the Dreamworld, I appreciate your perspective of deeming it to be not-real. But now, having descended that pathway created for you, I hope that this realness becomes as solid for you as for cats and humans and ghouls. Despite it being the best choice, we are dismayed that the thing was sent into the Dreamworld and is now running loose there."

"There?" asks Jake. "Don't you mean here? Isn't this all a dream?"

"This is light slumber," says Algernon. "Deeper dream lies below, beyond. And we need the both of you to help us find the thing that she sent there."

"This is silly," snorts Jake. "We're just going to wake up."

The cat looks at Sandy.

"Do you understand?" he asks her.

There is no threat in those words, or even in their tone, but Sandy reacts as if there is.

"Yes," she replies, ears down.

"Good. Explain it to him then, if you feel the need."

Sandy nods.

"We will meet here tonight," declares Algernon. "Sentries will be posted around your homes. Listen for their calls. Fall asleep as soon as you can after that, then make your way through the mist and down the ramp. The two of you will lead the way to this thing. And it will be dealt with."

***

They woke.

There was no sign of the cat, though its scent hung in the air. Overhead, the sun was covered by a cloud, but in roughly the same spot. They'd napped only minutes.

"Did you dream?" whined Jake. "Cave and cat and man?"

"I did."

"Was it real?"

"It was."

"Tonight?"

"Tonight."

***

A blur of movement, low in the grass. Something small, zipping here, zipping there. Start, stop, start, stop. It's checking, always checking.

Chipmunk!

Long ago, SHE had named it so, and the word had stuck. Like a mouse, but not. The stripe down its back is the giveaway. For Jake, the thing would be a decent two-bite meal, filling his belly. For a while, anyway. Butch, the immense Great Dane he knew, would have no problem swallowing it with a single gulp. Anything on the ground near Butch is doomed to be chomped, and quickly. Sandy, on the other hand, might comfortably stretch it into two meals, fiercely defending the leftovers until she could get down the rest.

It takes off again, triggering the instinct to chase, but Jake stops himself. He'd learned about chipmunks: too much effort to run down. Very agile, they always seem to be a short skitter away from some sort of refuge. Sure enough, that's where this one goes, diving into a convenient gap at the base of a tree.

And, of course, it goes into the roots. They are so tough to dig through and between. Not that he's allowed to do that. SHE scolds him when he digs holes anywhere, especially in his own yard. Sometimes, he does it anyway to play with her—though NEVER in the garden at the one end. And SHE knows he's playing. But Jake has to pick those moments carefully.

The urge to play is far away now, though. The chance—as slim as it is—of getting that chipmunk inspires Jake to try a new strategy: waiting for its head to pop up for a look. Settling down, he wonders what the tiny thing tastes like. SHE always keeps him well-fed for his breakfast and dinner, with snacks between. And at night, before bedtime, there are sometimes a few crunchy, salty pretzels.

Where?

Growing impatient, Jake creeps right up to the hole. And the more he stares at that little spot, the darker it seems to get. That particular hole is strange. Very strange. Almost…menacing.

And he hadn't caught it at first, but embedded within that shadowy blackness: a speck of yellow. He tries to make sense of the sight. If anything, there should be a brown chipmunk with a white and black stripe. That's it.

But, framed by the roots, the pattern of light within dark makes it look like an…

Eye?

It is an eye! And it blinks!

Jake recoils, growling, ready to—

***

"Jake."

Like the dream that it was, the danger faded. He was at home, and SHE was with him on the couch. The television continued to show uninteresting pictures of sand and rocks. Jake liked to watch dogs and horses and deer, even cats. But tonight's dull images, combined with the stuffy warmth, had put him to sleep.

23

Safe.

And being relaxed enough to fall asleep implied safety, but were they? Memories of recent dreams and recent reality collided, overlapping. That automatic, mindless safety associated with *home* was missing. He tried to distract himself from the disturbing thought.

Pictures.

That colorful window to the world now showed men riding atop some ugly horses.

Horses?

No, they weren't horses. SHE had named them something else, but the word was eluding him. Staring at the misshapen animals against the backdrop of sand, another memory competed for attention. He felt it was something significant.

Sandy?

Yes, it was something having to do with Sandy, but the sleep fog prevented him from latching onto it.

"Are you okay?" SHE asked.

Hearing concern in her voice, his tail thumped the couch in a half-wag.

"Want to go out?"

Out?

He did. Anyway, it was time for a final empty of his bladder, a final check of the property.

After a lazy stretch, he went through the kitchen and out the little door. The temperature was refreshing, blowing away the remaining fogginess. He shifted into patrol mode for a thorough circuit around the yard. All that he discovered was a newly fallen branch. A twig, really.

Then a breeze carried an odor past his nose.

Cat!

One was close. Perhaps right on the other side of the fence? He put his nose against a crack between two boards and took a great, snurfling sniff.

No.

It wasn't that close. Smells of cats reminded him that he had seen one today. A grey one with a white mark on his chest. With Sandy. He had met up with his little friend, and a cat had been there. Sandy had been wanting him to growl in a specific way. His throat was still sore from the repeated attempts.

Why?

With the breeze having died down, all was quiet except for the noise of cars moving along the streets of the neighborhood. Above the top of the fence, the moon was an oblong slash of brightness set against the dark sky. It was similar to something he'd seen recently…

Bird-not-bird!

THAT had been the start: a bright, yellow bird that wasn't a bird, both dead and alive at the same time. There one day, it had been gone the next. Then, Sandy and he had argued about it, and some sort of vibration had occurred. After that had come the nightmare of being trapped. An insubstantial and ungraspable thing, it had transformed into something real and solid. That awfulness, whatever it was, had appeared beside him on the porch, disguised to look perfectly like SHE did. But Sandy had sent it away by barking and growling, over and over and over.

That had been this morning, and the most horrible part of the whole affair that had lodged in his brain was the uncertainty. The thing had taken the form of SHE, the most wonderful constant of his entire life. And there had been thoughts of wanting to hurt Sandy, his most reliable friend. Such conflict had created mistrust and doubt where there had never been any.

The conclusion of the string of bizarre events had been this afternoon: Sandy and he falling asleep and having a dream with a grey cat in it. Jake had dreamed about Sandy many times, and cats occasionally. But he had never spoken to a cat before, and couldn't imagine a circumstance where he would want to. Despite that, his imaginary excursion had involved communication with, not only that cat, but a man as well. He tried to focus on their identities, but the names wouldn't come.

A cat yowled, cutting through the silence. Then a different cat, its voice pitched impossibly higher. Then, together, the overlapping set of wails raised the hair on Jake's back. Were they fighting over territory? Or food? Or—

Signal!

That must have been the signal that—

Algernon!

That was the cat's name. He needed to meet Sandy and Algernon. Down a ramp. In a cave. And the cave was in a dream, so he needed to fall asleep.

Silly.

Jake knew the concept of absurd, but not the word. In his mind, silly covered a lot, including the need to meet up with someone while sleeping. It made no sense, but he would try. If he succeeded, fine. If not, also fine.

The neighborhood quiet again, the yard clear, it was time for sleep anyway. He went inside.

***

Dim light, mist. It's disorienting to Jake, but familiar. This is where he'd been earlier, and is supposed to be now.

No.

This isn't the spot.

Down.

He remembers a wall with a hole and a ramp that goes down. Sandy would be there, and together they would…do…*something.* Exactly what isn't important at the moment. But what seems to be vital is to find that entrance.

The grey blankets everything, revealing no details. There is a memory of following cat-scent through the fog, but the ground holds no scent in any direction as he wanders. He stops to listen.

Nothing.

He is alone here, wherever *here* is.

There is no fear attached to that realization, just sadness. A feeling that he is letting Sandy down, and not for the first time. She always seems to be smarter, always knows things. She's probably waiting for him now. Waiting and wondering if poor, stupid Jake can do one, simple thing. Growing angry at himself, and with no one to witness his frustration, there's no need to hold it in.

"No!"

The bark echoes back, off of something.

Ears perk up as he turns his head to the left, lets loose with another.

"Yes!"

The wall must be in that direction. A few steps, another bark.

Closer…

Relieved, he keeps going. The shape of a wall appears out of the gloom. Along the base there's a hole, too small for him and reeking of cat. Passing that by, he goes a little further.

Here!

This is the doorway, and with the much more pleasant scent of trees and earth, flowers and grass, squirrels and chipmunks: the park.

As Jake winds his way down to the right, his thoughts clear. Memories of the previous visit return. Despite knowing what awaits him at the bottom, he's awed by the vastness of the open space, the ceiling so high that he can barely pick it out. But more breathtaking is the column of fire burning at the far end. Centered in a huge, golden dish, flames blossom upward. Twisting and intertwined, there is an impression that it is under control. But what fire can ever be tamed?

Near the base of that conflagration, speaking with each other again, are the cat and the oddly dressed man.

Algernon and Kaman-Thah.

There's no sign of Sandy.

Unsure of whether to wait for her or not, he saunters slowly toward the pair, exploring as he goes. Both of the long sides of the cavern are lined with human-sized statues carved from black, glossy stone. Mounted onto the wall on either side of the figures, small flames burn. Heading to the right, he finds that they are mainly of men and women, but a couple he cannot identity. One looks like a dog, vaguely, but the texture of the skin is different than the rest. Captured in stone, there is nevertheless the suggestion of being dead and rotting.

One after the other, Jake looks, sniffs, moves on. Closer to the source of the conversation, he is able to hear some of the words.

"It could be," says Algernon. "I cannot say."

"Her power against that one would be limited," sighs the priest. "Although deception and illusion can be effective if used properly."

"If that worst case scenario does come to pass... Mouse in the nose is not mouse on the tongue, but we have been assured that the prize it would seek is well-hidden."

The man nods.

A look back shows no sign of Sandy. Jake turns his attention to the next statue—and wishes he hadn't. More than any of the others, this one seems to have a cloud of *evil* clinging to it. The material is the same glossy black, with the form of a tall man, but light bounces off of it, or is absorbed, creating shadows somehow darker than the stone itself.

As Jake stares at it, he's not entirely sure that the statue is supposed to be a man. The stone seems to shift and flow, becoming different people, different...things. Monstrous creatures. It has three legs, then back to two. Wings form and flap, then dissolve. Two eyes become one, then none. The head splits and transforms, with a wreath of snakes sprouting from between the shoulders.

No!

He looks away, clamps his eyes shut, and waits. Then, a careful glance back shows...the shape of a tall man.

Relieved, he decides that this is a good spot to mark. The lack of smells to that point had become more than a little disconcerting. The entire floor that he had covered, all of the statues:

nothing. Even the little fires burn without smoke, though he detects the remnants of a floral scent hanging in the air.

It's time to make this more like my yard.

He starts to lift his leg—

"JAKE!"

Catching himself in time, he turns to find Sandy running toward him, her stubby legs churning furiously. When moving at speed, her light brown fur flaps and waves a bit. With her eyes fixed on the statue behind him, she comes to a stop a good distance away.

"Come here!" she hisses.

Glad to leave the ominous chunk of stone, he trots over to her. Algernon and Kaman-Thah begin a discussion, but this time he can't make out any of their words.

"What's wrong?" asks Jake.

"You can't pee here!"

"Why not? We're not inside." He looks around, up. "Well, maybe we are. Sort of. Wait. We are in a dream, right?"

"Yes."

"That's what I thought. I can do whatever I want in a dream."

"You can," she allows. "But..." There's a shake of her head. "Do you remember the dead bird-thing?"

"Of course. It was yellow. And very bad."

"But it wasn't a bird, was it?"

That much was undeniable. A normal dead bird would not cause all the trouble that this one had.

"No," says Jake.

"Okay. Now, think of *that*"— she lifts her nose toward the statue— "the same way. It's neither a statue nor a man. And

30

marking it would be very, very bad. At the very least you have to think of this place as Kaman-Thah's home. What would Linda say if you—"

"Who?"

"Linda. Your pack leader."

"SHE?"

"Her name is Linda, Jake."

"Oh. Right. I've heard that. I just don't think—"

"That's right," barks Sandy. "You don't think."

Holding back a whimper, he hangs his head.

"Oh, Jake. I'm sorry. It's not just you. Nearly all dogs let instinct guide their every move. Running and playing, sniffing and peeing, are all fine, but there's more to life. Our awake world can be confusing, but just because Linda guides you through the craziness doesn't mean you're not equals. The two of you are a team. Right?"

He nods, reluctantly, as the words sink in.

"There's so much potential in you. You're young enough to change the way you act. Make new habits. Be less impulsive. Think."

She finishes with slow, apologetic wags of her tail.

Her speech stirs something within him. It's always been there: a feeling that there is more that he may be missing out on, but doesn't know where to look, or whom to ask. Or, perhaps most importantly, which questions to ask.

"Well," sighs Jake. "We're here, like we're supposed to be. Right?"

"Right."

"And we're going with Algernon?"

31

"We are. And?"

"The bird-thing! We have to find it because…"

Sandy gives Jake a moment, then prompts him, "Because I—"

"Because you sent it here!" exclaims Jake. "How did you do that?"

"The chant of Not-Real. I was trying to teach you that this afternoon."

"My throat still hurts from that." Jake probes for the soreness. "Wait. It doesn't."

"Because you're dreaming. This is how you usually think of yourself. That sore throat is temporary and new, so it didn't become part of this version of you."

"How do you know so many things, Sandy?"

"We can talk about that later. We should go now."

But, staring at the pair awaiting them, she doesn't move.

"Jake, this is a new place, not just for you, but for all dogs. We'll see many strange things. I can't say what will happen, but need to warn you." Her voice drops to a whisper. "Watch Algernon. Awake or dreaming, cats have their own agenda."

"Agenda?"

"Plans. They have their own plans, and we have no way of knowing if they're good for us or bad for us."

"You don't trust him?"

"I don't trust any cat."

The smile on Kaman-Thah's face is a wonderful, welcoming sight for Jake. As bewildering as the whole situation is, and despite the fresh rebuke from Sandy, his wags can't be stopped.

The priest bows slightly before speaking.

"My friends, it is an honor to welcome you back. Your presence here is unique, as you may have gathered."

"You've made it clear that we are the first," replies Sandy.

"Yes. I am pleased that dreamers such as yourselves will have the opportunity to experience the lands below. Your perspectives will be valuable. If you would grant me time at the end of your journey, I would like to learn from you and make an entry in our archives. Or perhaps on subsequent—"

"THAT decision," interjects Algernon, "has not yet been made."

The priest's smile fades.

"Isn't this world of common dream meant for all?" asks Sandy.

"All for whom a doorway exists," replies Kaman-Thah. His lips twitch as if he wants to say more, but a scowl from the cat stops him. There is a frown on the face of the priest as he continues. "Beyond that, the entrance must be discovered by the individuals and the choice to enter must be made. Some choose not to."

"I don't know why anyone wouldn't want to," comments Jake, more to Sandy, but loud enough for all.

"It may have something to do with the company," she suggests, glaring at Algernon.

The cat matches her gaze.

"Are you prepared to find the creature you sent here?" he asks.

"As prepared as we can be," she growls. "How did it even get to our neighborhood?"

The cat shrugs.

"Through a hole, crack, fissure, rift. Pick whichever term you like. The essence of the universe is far from perfect. The thing found a flaw and took advantage."

"Yes, but did that flaw occur naturally? Or was it deliberately produced?"

"That's not pertinent."

"I believe it is," counters Sandy. "And it's possible to get that answer. If you would give me some time, I could—"

"Time is a precious commodity and it cannot be spent on solving the riddle of how it broke through the veils. The thing is here. We need to find it here. Now. Before its lead grows too large."

"Fine," grumbles Sandy. "On our first visit, you used the term Shabh-lith. Tell us about it."

"That one was dispensed with."

"You said as much. But what was it? Tell us *something*. So far, we have *nothing* to go on."

"According to our history, tens of thousands of years ago Shabh-lith found its way to the waking world." Then, pointedly, he adds, "How that happened was not recorded."

"And, like this event, it was banished from there to here?" asks Sandy.

"Yes."

"By a dog?" asks Jake.

"By a man," replies the cat. "Beings of all types—cats, humans, ghouls—suffered greatly as it killed, then vanished. Again, and again. Eventually, the cats of that time did confront it. The final campaign required an enormous force and cost many lives. We are prepared to pay that price again, but hope that fewer innocents are affected."

Following along, one crucial detail doesn't make sense to Jake.

"Didn't you say that it's dead?" he asks.

"That one is. But as with any living thing, there are always others of a similar sort. Or a worse sort."

"And you *still* have not described its appearance," huffs Sandy.

"That one looked more like a mole than anything else," snaps the cat. "But much larger: twice the size of any human. And it had a way of blending into the scenery—the trees and rocks—so as to be nearly invisible."

Sandy shakes her head and snorts a laugh. Then another. The tension having grown, Jake appreciates the attempt to lighten the mood. Smiling, he wants to join her, but doesn't understand what she is laughing about.

"Thank you," says Sandy. "If I may sum this up: We're in search of something that may or may not be visible, and when it can be seen, may or may not look like a giant mole."

Tail thrashing, Algernon's shoulders droop.

"That is correct," he mutters.

"And you have no idea where it is?"

"No," says the cat, head down. "Its entrance was notable, but indefinite. We could not pin down an exact location."

"Then this is useless. If we can't even see it, there's no hope at all of finding it within eight hours."

At that, Algernon sits up straight.

"Ah, but you do not realize how much faster time flows in the world below. You can easily be there for weeks during a single night of dreaming."

"Weeks are certainly better," concedes Sandy. "Will that be enough?"

"There's no way to know." More confidently, he continues, "But Jake has become linked to it and will know how to find it."

That's news to Jake.

"How?" he asks, head tilting. "You say that like I know all about it. But I don't know anything, except that it's not a yellow bird and it's not dead. I went all through here. I don't smell it. There's nothing except for the three of you and some flowers."

"The creature you seek certainly did not enter this chamber," says Kaman-Thah. "Due to the actions of your companion, it could not have. But flowers… There have never been any in this place." His eyes lighting up, he asks, "Incense, do you mean?" He inhales through his nose. "Do either of you smell anything?"

Sandy sniffs, shakes her head.

"I smell nothing," says Algernon. "Is there something wrong?"

Pointing at a censer of polished silver, the priest walks over to a wooden stand near the column of flame and returns with it. With every bit of the surface curved to some degree or other, the craftsmanship is unequalled. Removing the top, he kneels down to let Jake smell within, as shiny and spotless as the exterior.

"That's it," confirms Jake. "Like flowers, but sweeter."

"Jasmine," says Kaman-Thah, capping it and standing. "But five millennia have passed since it was last used."

Algernon raises an eyebrow.

"Truly, that is impressive," remarks the cat.

"It's just my nose," says Jake.

"Will it be too powerful?" Sandy asks the priest.

"Perhaps," he replies, then turns to Jake. "My friend, this will be your first venture in the world below. Many new things await. Many new odors. Possibly too many, possibly too strong. I cannot prepare you, but I can offer you a warning. Your humble nose may be more of a hindrance than a help. You will need to take care. Go slowly. And believe in yourself."

It's not the words, but the manner in which they're delivered, that gets through.

"I need to be careful?" asks Jake.

"Very," replies the priest.

"And think?" he adds, glancing at Sandy.

"Always."

"Okay. I'll do that."

"We're wasting time," says Sandy. "We should get started."

With a nod, Kaman-Thah leads them around the tremendous dish that holds the flame. Behind it, an opening in the wall reveals a wide staircase leading down. Torches are mounted at regular intervals on the left, a string of dots swallowed by the darkness, the bottom indeterminably far away.

The dogs walk forward, but Sandy notices that Algernon isn't moving.

"Are you coming?" she asks the cat. "You're supposed to be leading us."

"I will meet you there. I cannot… I must go a different way."

"Of course you do," murmurs Sandy, but only loudly enough for Jake to hear.

Seven hundred.

According to Kaman-Thah, that's the number of steps. But that value means nothing to Jake. It's too big. Maybe Sandy is keeping track, but he isn't.

37

The stone has a rough texture similar to the ramp at the entrance to the cavern, allowing Jake to trust his grip. But that slope had been very dog-friendly. This staircase is made for two legs, longer strides. In other words, for humans. Like…

Linda.

The name is an uncomfortable presence in his mind, a concept that he's coming to terms with. The one he had known his whole life as SHE is now Linda.

Stopping to rest, he looks back to find Sandy. She's pausing also, the trip down more taxing on her shorter legs. Looking past her, he can no longer see the top, though the path had not run in a straight line. There had been gentle curves in both directions.

Down, dots of torches mark the way to a bottom that remains obscured by distance. The small flames illuminate little more than the natural-looking rock of the steps. Unlike the gigantic room above, this ceiling is set at a more typical height. On the left the wall has been a constant, but on the right there is empty space. One curious look into that abyss was all that Jake needed. He made a point to stay next to the nice, dependably-solid wall.

When Sandy begins to move again, Jake waits for her. Their wordless descent had become, not spooky, but uncomfortable. They had never *spoken* when awake, instead communicating with barks and wags. And though such expressions had conveyed plenty enough meaning his entire life, the ease of talking or thinking or whatever is happening here makes Jake want to take advantage of it.

"Sandy, who is in your pack?" he asks when she makes it down to his step.

"Hmm?"

"I have…Linda. Who is the man who brings you to the park?"

"That's Sam. Sam and Ivy. Just the two of them."

"Ivy is the one with long hair? It's been a long time since I've seen her."

"Her hair is all gone now," says Sandy quietly. "She's sick."

"Will she get better?"

"I don't know," she says, hanging her head.

Before Jake can figure out how to respond, she stands tall again.

"Let's go," she tells him. "We're almost at the bottom."

They begin moving, with Jake pausing every two or three steps to stay near his smaller companion. For a while, he focuses on the stone underpaw. Then, after what seems to be a long time, he realizes that it's brighter than it had been. A look up confirms it: an opening in the rock through which the stairs had taken them, and a view of a sunlit clearing.

Excited by the prospect, he trots down the last dozens of steps. But Sandy calls out before he goes very far.

"Jake!"

He stops, looks back.

"Remember what the priest said? With your nose, you need to be careful."

The prospect of a parklike setting beckons, but Jake is able to contain the urge and wait for Sandy. At last, her toenails touch down on the stone floor. They cover the few dog-lengths to the exit and look out at a natural tapestry that contrasts sharply with the sterile passage they descended.

Outside, the clearing looks to have been trampled by many feet or paws. Beyond that: endless, darkly colored trees. A grey-green fungus covers many of the thick trunks, and moss droops from their branches. Even the rocks that can be seen are colored with a living carpet of varying shades. Only some hardy shrubs wedged between the many roots look the least bit familiar, but they sport a less-than-inviting set of thorns.

Right at the edge, no odors penetrate within. It's as if they're looking out through a closed window.

"You didn't smell anything the whole time on the stairs, did you?" asks Sandy.

"No. It was like where we started from." Inhaling deeply, he adds, "And still nothing right here."

"I think that'll change as soon as we go out. Get ready."

With a nod, Jake takes a step. And a breath.

Like a slap, it hits: the transition from a total vacuum to a new world exploding with odors. Must and mildew strike first, blanketing his nose completely. A sneeze clears that out, but only temporarily. Humid air rushes back in, bringing other aromas along: normal, expected ones of earth and stone and water. And…creatures. Things he has no knowledge of. Good, bad, large, small, … He can't tell. There are many of them, though. The area is overrun with whatever they are.

Overwhelmed, there's a jerk backwards as he almost retreats into the safety of the scentless cave.

But he doesn't.

Eyes shut, stubbornly holding his ground, he sifts through the nasal onslaught, cataloging all he can.

There's Sandy, of course.

Cats. Cats have been by here recently.

People. Many people. Too many to count.

Mice. Or rats. He can tell one individual from another, but hasn't learned yet how to distinguish the species.

Birds.

The thought of one bird in particular is what anchors him. He's here, in this strange place, to track down that bird-thing. Concentrating, he tries to single out that specific odor.

"Is he alright?" asks a voice.

Again and again, Jake tries. But it's not there.

"I'm not sure," says another.

Sandy. That was Sandy's voice. Who else... Algernon?

Blinking, looking around, Jake sees that the grey cat is indeed there, though he doesn't smell quite the same.

Sandy nuzzles Jake. "Are you okay?" she asks.

Staring at the cat, Jake pokes his nose toward it and sniffs again. Whatever had been odd, or off, is gone.

"Jake?" prompts Sandy.

"Yes?"

"Are you okay?"

"I am now. But so far, I can't smell it."

"Here, I would be extremely surprised if you could," says Algernon. "There is a large population of Zoogs in the vicinity. Their odor dominates everything."

Hearing the word, Jake looks to Sandy for understanding, but she only shrugs.

"Zoogs?" he asks.

"Of the creatures known to you, they resemble rats more than anything else. They should leave us alone, but will be watching for the next day or so, while we are within their territory."

41

"How do we start?" asks Sandy. "There's no point is wandering around aimlessly until Jake picks up the scent. Do you have any theories as to where it may be?"

"I do, but in opposite directions. And though the two of you have no knowledge of this realm, I do not wish to speak the names of those places. I strongly prefer to not influence Jake in any way. He needs to find the trail and tell us where to go."

"And when we get there? Three is not an army."

"We are only scouting. We will receive support at the proper time."

After a pause, Sandy offers a short wag of satisfaction and looks at Jake. Then Algernon does also. A pressure builds in the young dog. Then guilt takes hold, as if he's done something wrong. But he knows he hasn't. And they're looking at him, waiting.

What do they want? I don't know!

"I'm sorry I can't smell it," he whines. "There are too many other things here."

"He's right," says Sandy. "We need to get up higher." Spinning around, she gapes at the cave from which they emerged. Her head tilts. "But there were hundreds of steps…"

As she looks at Algernon for an answer, Jake makes the connection. Having walked down so far, there should be ground to contain those stairs. And it should be right there. And it is, sort of. The entrance is in a mound of rock, but that mass of stone doesn't rise even as high as his own house, back in the awake world. The surrounding trees tower over it.

"The stairs are a manifestation of will," explains Algernon. "They could have been situated anywhere, but those who came first chose to conceal them within that tor."

"All right," says Sandy. "Let's skip the metaphysics lesson for right now. Are there any nearby hills where the trees thin out? A place where the winds can carry odors down to Jake?"

"No. The Enchanted Wood and surrounding lands are relatively flat and covered in dense vegetation. Openings in the trees such as this are scarce." He looks around, then up. His eyes lock onto something.

A black speck floating high above, it's either too distant or too small for Jake to discern.

"A change in altitude can be arranged, however," adds the cat. "We only need a sacrifice."

Those words stained with threat, Jake recalls the warning from Sandy. Keeping an eye on Algernon, he's startled to see a fawn stroll out of the trees. It stops and stands calmly, oblivious to the audience of predators. Jake doesn't consider the cat's approach disarming in the least, but there is no reaction from the prey. Standing beneath it, Algernon jumps upward. An expert slash across the throat unleashes a torrent of red.

The attack breaks whatever spell the young deer had been under. A gurgled cry and three shaky steps are all that it can manage before crumpling. The teeth chatter when it hits. Though delicate and tiny, the sound sends a chill down Jake's spine.

"Feel free to have some," says Algernon. "It won't matter if a few mouthfuls are missing."

Latching onto the fur near the wound, the cat yanks his head back violently. As the young, thin hide tears, blood flows freely with the final pulses of the heart.

Jake is mesmerized. Not having had any success with his rare attempts at hunting, he's never had an opportunity to eat

43

something freshly dead. The thought of meat so raw and warm is very appealing, but the newness of the situation gives him pause.

Sandy?

And now, she's helping Algernon. A tug of war between dog and cat exposes the tender meat under the fur. She sticks her snout in and takes a bite.

There's really not that much blood, but it seems as if every bit of it is on the small dog. With her body so close to the ground, it's easy for a misstep to spatter it all over. And her jaws and throat are the worst, a pure, slick red. There's a bath in her future for sure...

"Jake."

Sandy's voice brings him back.

"Jake, there aren't going to be any bowls of food. And we'll be here for days or weeks. We're going to have to eat mice and rabbits. And deer."

"Listen to her," chimes in Algernon after swallowing a mouthful. "It can be a terrible ordeal to lose the innocence of a kitten, but harsh reality is a ravenous, unstoppable beast, ever on the hunt. And it relishes devouring the traits of youth. You must escape from your shell in order to grow." Returning to the kill, he tears off another piece.

Hunger in Jake's belly forces his legs to move. Right beside the carcass, the metallic smell of blood blots out all else. Sandy steps back to give him some room.

Had he grown used to the sight, or did the carnivore within surface? Regardless, the torn meat and blood seem perfectly normal now. But, instead of biting off a morsel, he licks it.

Disgusting!

As he retreats, coughing and gagging, his lashing tongue tries to rid itself of the acrid coating. Dry heaves take over but bring up nothing.

"I'm sorry," says Sandy as she walks over to Jake. "It is an acquired taste. Algernon, this one is different from what I recall. Is that because you summoned it?"

Leaping off the deer, he joins the dogs.

"Correct. That taste is my preference. In the future we should eat separately."

"See, Jake? You'll like rabbits much better. Trust me."

The taste wearing off, he gives a tentative nod.

A shadow darkens the area, briefly.

"Perhaps it's just as well he has nothing in his stomach," says Algernon, looking up. "As naive as he is, I believe this next episode will be even more unnerving."

The shadow returns, and Jake is astounded to see what is causing it: immense wings.

It lands with a fluttering thump. Much bigger, much more muscular than the hawks Jake has seen, the bird cannot be categorized as elegant. But, despite an awkwardness and a dull collage of black and white feathers, it conveys a certain majesty in its movements.

"We welcome your presence, Blessed Flyer," says Algernon.

"Your words imply a need," squawks the bird.

"A small thing."

"Speak it. I hunger."

"Carry this larger one as high as you can, stay up for a time, then return him unharmed."

The bird studies Jake, then the carcass.

There is a caw of agreement.

"Jake," says Algernon, "this noble vulture will carry you high into the air so that you can locate our quarry."

"Carry?" he yelps, looking up at the tops of the trees. "How high?"

"Very. You must be brave. You are the only one who can do this. Above the treetops, you'll have access to odors from a much broader region. They will be very faint, but you will need to use your mind as well as your nose. As you sift the air for odors, think back to the thing you found in the waking world. Find the direction we need to go."

When Algernon motions to the vulture, it hops closer. Jake stands his ground—until the beak opens and the miasma of a recent meal wafts out.

"Stay still!"

The reprimand anchors him in place, but Jake can't do anything about his trembling as the beak clamps onto the scruff of his neck. The hold is firm, but not painful, as it lifts him up slightly then releases him.

"Squirm too much and I'll drop you," it says. "And when you splatter, I get to eat up all the bits!" Throwing its head back, it laughs: a single, loud croak.

Wings spread, the bird uses a hop and a flap to get the height needed to grab Jake by the scruff with one of its claws. Needles dig in, and he's jerked upward. More flapping, then the second set of talons connect. Every beat elicits a chorus of stings. Whining and struggling, the bird's warning flashes back. The thought of being dropped grants him the will to ignore the pain. Then he sees treetops that, seconds before, had been far overhead. Now, his paws practically graze them!

Jake's eyes slam shut as he works to control the fear and focus on what needs to be done.

Find the right way to go.

The sooner he does that, the sooner he can get back to solid earth. But each flap sweeps the bird's odor into his nostrils, preventing him from smelling anything else. The short times between, however, he does begin to detect other odors. Trees and Zoogs from below are there, but not as strong. Water—a stream or river or lake—becomes prominent.

Minutes go by as he struggles to identify odors from the snippets that come through between blasts of bird. Frustration builds, and with it, some nerve. And as he screws up his courage enough to ask the bird to stop its relentless flapping for a short while, it does.

They glide, silently.

The suspension in air is something Jake has never before experienced, but is such an alien state that there is nothing in his memories with which to compare. For him, the dead quietness is the more remarkable aspect. Back in his home, even during the darkest hours of night in the dead of winter, there is always something to hear: a creak of the house, a car going by outside. At this moment: only the faintest whisper of breeze. Tempted to open his eyes, he cracks them—

Don't!

There's no point in being more terrified than he already is. Keeping lids tightly sealed, the claws a steady pain, no distracting sounds, and the odor of the vulture being cleanly swept behind

47

them as they fly along, there's finally gets a chance to do what he's there for. A deep inhale through his nose provides a multitude of aromas to review. Skipping anything well-known and wholesome, he tries to find that distinctive odor. But there's nothing.

He tries again… Nothing.

And nothing.

And more nothing.

Through closed eyelids, the warmth and brightness of the sun shifting around, he can tell they've been circling. One set of talons relax slightly before pinching down again and Jake wonders how much longer the bird can hold him.

"Well?" it asks, as if reading his thoughts. "Have we been up here long enough?"

"Almost," barks Jake, the unease induced by his current, unnatural position easily covering the stress lying to this creature that held his life in its claws.

Fighting through a panic of possible failure, thinking back, he recalls finding that mystifying dead-not-dead bird-thing. He'd been about to taste it, but a very bad feeling had intervened.

Holding onto the memory of that badness, he draws in another great lungful of air and picks up—

Something!

Something that tickles the back of his nose in a familiar and frightful way.

That's it!

Trying to get a fix on the direction, his head whips left and right.

That way! Behind! Away from the sun!

Excited, his thrashing is too much for the vulture. One claw lets go.

"We're done!" it announces.

Wings fold and they dive. The single set of needles sink in, bringing a pain that can't be brushed aside. And at perhaps the worst moment, Jake's resolve wanes: He opens his eyes.

They're spiraling in, the ground rushing up at him much faster than he could ever imagine. His howls of terror are swept away by the wind before they even reach his ears.

He catches a glimpse of a river cutting a swath through a sea of trees.

Lower, there are only treetops and the clearing from which they'd left.

Then, the dead fawn, Sandy, Algernon.

A slowing, leveling off, brings a glimmer of relief, but only a glimmer.

The bird lets him go, and he's falling!

Crack!

Jake lands squarely on the ribcage of the deer—viscera squirting out through the flesh that had been torn open—then bounces off and rolls.

"Perfect," caws the vulture as it touches down.

Laying on his side, Jake has an unobstructed view of the bird attacking the liver, ripping off and swallowing a great hunk. Looking away, he can't help but see other bloody bits scattered about.

It's too much. The full weight of that spinning descent hits. His body reacts, trying to vomit forcefully from the very pit of his gut. But with nothing having gone in, nothing comes out. At last, the spasms end.

On shaky legs, he stands. Turning his back on the messy feasting, he ambles toward Sandy and Algernon. They meet him halfway.

"Did you find the thing?" the cat asks eagerly. "Do you have a bearing?

Jake hears the words, but as if through a fog. He works to make sense of them.

"Give him a minute," snarls Sandy.

Jake sits down.

"Take your time," she tells him.

He nods, concentrates. Eventually, the world slows, stabilizes. An image forms, solidifies.

"Away from the sun," he yelps, throat sore from the heaving. "Toward a river."

Algernon looks up to the late afternoon sun behind a cloud, then gazes east.

"Somehow," he sighs, "that is not the least bit surprising."

With Algernon having confirmed his satisfaction with Jake's findings, the cat takes the lead. A number of openings in the trees are visible on the eastern edge of the small field, but instead of going straight east, he guides them northeast. Neither dog objects. Jake doesn't even notice. Still rattled, the only effort he makes is to keep his paws in motion. He tags along last, behind Sandy, his slowed pace now a better match to the natural strides of the others.

Trod by many feet over countless years, the trail is clean and easy to follow. Fungus grows on most of the dark trunks, and when the lowering sun is masked by a cloud—or more the case, that the foliage is particularly dense overhead—that natural coating can be seen to glow with a soft, yellow-green light.

After a short time, a stream cuts across their way. A pair of sturdy logs set firmly next to each other provide easy access to the other bank, but Algernon abruptly turns them left, into the trees. The water tempts Jake, babbling to him of its coolness. So close, it unfortunately flows at the bottom of a ravine with steep sides, too deep to jump out of.

Off the path, it's not too difficult for any of the three to maneuver, but Jake could see larger dogs—and obviously people—having problems going where the cat takes them. They need to squeeze under fallen trees or between square stones. For Jake, the ones that are stacked suggest walls or fences, but there are hardly any remnants standing. Some pieces that seem to have been connected in the past lie far apart.

Once getting through one final hole there's a wonderful sight: a pool of water. It's not very big at all, but a sense—or perhaps an aroma—of purity emanates from it. Another pleasing detail is the ability to plainly see the sky through a break in the trees above the pool. Such a thing had been rare since the clearing in which they had started.

"Drink your fill," Algernon tells them, then perches on the bank and begins gently lapping. Sandy joins him.

Seeing no need to be delicate, Jake wades straight in and takes great gulps. The first is enough for him to feel a difference, soothing his throat. He had been getting hungry as well, but the water also helps with that. Inspired, he dips his head down. Immersed, the aching in his neck from the vulture's claws fades.

Taking the weight off his legs, he floats and looks around. A steady flow of water emerges from a rock wall at the far end of the pool. Running down, it fills the small, bowl-shaped area, overflowing to become the source of the stream.

Restored, Jake bounds out. Laying down on a bed of moss, he wiggles around on his back before springing to his feet and giving a great shake of his whole body. Droplets fly, spraying the other two. Neither seems to mind, especially when his entire face erupts into a smile.

"That's better," he says.

"The water has healing properties," explains Algernon. "Years and years ago, the efficacy was greater." He shuts his eyes, as if reliving a memory. "This was a thriving town, much like Ulthar is today. In fact, the survivors from here, having learned the error of their ways, established that other place." He opens his eyes and waves a paw vaguely southward.

"I was wondering about these stone blocks," comments Sandy. "The structures don't appear to have simply fallen down from great age. The end seems to have been violent. Do you know what happened?"

"The gods do not look kindly on certain actions. Repeated warnings went unheeded."

"But what, specifically?"

The cat's tail writhes for a few moments before he speaks.

"They killed a cat," he says.

Thirst sated, they make their way back and cross the makeshift bridge. Though the logs aren't secured together at all, it's plenty sturdy for their light weight. On the opposite bank, Algernon keeps them on the path as it turns right and stays parallel to the water. With each step downstream, the ravine seems to deepen, the burbling at the bottom farther away. Jake sees the wisdom of having detoured up to the pool for a drink, the only point granting easy access.

An hour of walking becomes two. The sun sinking, phosphorescent fungi provide plenty enough light under the canopy to allow them to keep going.

No longer fighting through the haze he had been in, Jake's senses come alive again. In particular, he takes note of the many things stirring in the woods. Some of the movements he can guess at, occasionally getting visual confirmation of a bird or squirrel or mouse. But those small things make no effort to disguise their movements. They dart or hop, then wait, then go on.

There are definitely other things though, things that make an effort to hide behind the trunks. Treading furtively, they make far less noise than a mouse, but enough. Zoogs, he guesses. Their collective odor is a constant, wafting around, blotting out nearly all else.

The stream that had been only inches across at its origin now courses through a chasm far too wide to leap. Many, smaller trickles of water had contributed to that main flow. Some of those creeks came with their own log bridges, while others required a trip down to the bottom of a gully, then a clamber back up.

A third hour of walking finally brings a change. They had been on relatively flat ground, the scenery at any given moment basically the same as it had ten, or twenty, minutes previous. But now, they begin to descend.

Slowly, their journey downward brings them closer to the water. Though that healing pool is far behind them, the liquid yet flows clear here. Searching the edge for an easy way to get down for a drink, Jake is caught off guard when he looks up: The trees end. Beyond that is a river, and easy access to the stream where it merges with the much larger flow.

"This is the River Oukranos," says Algernon. "We've come far enough today and will sleep here tonight."

Out of the trees, the twilight sky is a dark blue, but losing color rapidly. Jake can tell that the path turns left, downriver. He's curious as to what is ahead, but satisfied to know that they'll be exploring—

What?

The realization seems to hit Sandy at the same time. As they look at each other she voices exactly what he had been thinking.

"We're going to sleep? *While* we're asleep?"

The cat jiggles its whiskers.

"I apologize for laughing, but even in the current circumstances I am amused by that reaction."

The dogs wait patiently, somewhat confused, but not offended, by another round of whisker movement, capped off by a slow blink.

"Yes," says Algernon. "The mind needs consistency in order to function and navigate through dream correctly, be it cat or human, dog or ghoul."

"Or Zoog?" asks Sandy, looking at Jake.

"They're all around us," he says.

"And they will continue to monitor our progress. But to answer your question: Yes, to an extent. Zoogs live by their own rhythm, mainly diurnal. They are an integral and unique part of this world, and only this one. With no counterpart in your waking world, they do whatever Zoogs do, and in their own time."

"YOUR waking world?" growls Sandy.

"Forgive me. I meant to say *our*. I was only trying to emphasize the novelty of this place for the two of you."

Sandy nods, though Jake glimpses her forehead wrinkle briefly.

It is at that instant that Jake's stomach announces, to all, how empty it is.

"Let's have dinner," proposes the cat. "We all must be hungry by now. Sandy, for some reason I am expecting that you know what to do."

"Only willpower is needed?" she asks.

"That is all," says Algernon.

"Are you ready, Jake?"

"I sure am. Not deer, though?"

"Not deer," Sandy assures him. "Watch that bush."

This area, at the junction of the two water sources, is one of the few places in the forest that has undergrowth, and it's from beneath one of those shrubs that a rabbit materializes. Jake launches after it immediately. The thing heads downriver, along the path, and seems to be separating from Jake, but does a U-turn and comes back toward its pursuer. It nearly makes it past the dog, but superb reflexes and an athletic lunge allows Jake to clamp onto the neck. Hunger takes over, and there's a crunch as his jaws tighten. It goes limp.

The adrenaline of the chase coursing through him, he trots back and drops it in front of Sandy.

"Now what?" he asks.

"We eat it. Just like the deer, rip it open and eat."

The thought of doing that doesn't disturb him, but it's so…different. Every meal-memory Jake has is of his pack leader, Linda, providing for him. And most everything she'd ever given him had been tasty, except for some pungent, rubbery slices she had named *oranges*. Those? Yuck!

But meat was a different matter. He'd never met a chunk of meat he hadn't enjoyed, raw or cooked. And, Sandy had seemed to think earlier that he'd like rabbit.

Working alone, she tries to enlarge the one hole in the rabbit's throat that Jake had punched. And, as he watches her struggle, that small amount of blood in his mouth consciously registers. And it's good.

"Jake! Help me with this!"

Salivating, he does. After the work of tugging and tearing through the fur, Jake gets to taste rabbit for the first time.

And he likes it.

The dawn brings light, but no sun. With the river cutting through the woods, the trees on the other side, as high as the ones on this, would normally block sight of it for a while on any day. On this morning, a thick blanket of grey clouds looks impenetrable, keeping the temperature down as well. Jake sniffs the breeze, but there doesn't seem to be any rain forthcoming.

All three had spent the night together tucked into a crack in the rock that above the riverbank. The little hideaway had been cool to start, but their collective body heat had warmed it during the course of the night. More welcome for Jake had been the thin layer of moss, providing more cushioning than bare stone.

It hadn't been as comfortable as a couch, though.

Stretching the morning laziness away, he remembers that he actually *is* home. He is on the floor of the sleeping room right now, SHE/Linda above him, in the bed. All he has to do is wake up…

"Jake!" comes Sandy's voice from the river's edge. "Algernon!"

The pair rush to meet her.

She points at prints in the moist earth that are like nothing Jake has ever seen. A quick scent is all he needs. Sandy already knows.

"It must be Zoogs," she says. "They were here during the night? This close?"

"As I said yesterday, they are, and will remain so. They're nothing to worry about, however. Cats and Zoogs have a treaty."

"And without the treaty, they would attack?"

Algernon seems to consider his answer before replying.

"It depends. Zoogs are not complicated creatures, but they have a complex society. They do like to be entertained and rely on a strong oral tradition. The ones who watch us will ensure that all of the details of our journey are recorded for generations to come."

"But we haven't done anything yet," says Jake. "Just some walking."

"There was your trip up, high into the sky. Such a thing is likely to never have been seen by any of them before."

"I was trying to forget," admits Jake. "I really don't want to do that again."

"And you shouldn't have to. There will be other options for gaining the altitude that you need."

Jake nods but can't help but wonder if those options will be any better.

Breakfast of a couple of squirrels isn't as good as dinner had been. The skin is much easier to tear apart, but the meat has a sharp taste that Jake doesn't like. Sandy also prefers rabbit, and promises to stick to that for the most part.

"But I am going to mix it up from time to time," she warns him. "You should take advantage of this and try a variety of animals as long as you're here."

As he had done the previous night, Algernon had kept well away from the dogs while dining. This morning, behind a clump of tall grass along the bank further downriver, a slew of tiny squeals that had been heard at the start of his feasting were silenced, one by one.

Afterward, the cat meets them at the mouth of the stream.

"We'll have plenty to drink along the way," he remarks. "And food won't be an issue, either."

"Where are we going?" asks Sandy.

"East."

"Can you be a little more specific?"

"There are no roads in this part of the world, but this trail is fine. It will take us slightly out of the way as the river flows north, but the trip will be easy going. We'll pass some towns—"

"But how far?" snaps Sandy.

"That's for Jake's nose to tell us, isn't it?"

There are hours of plodding, Algernon ever in the lead. The scenery had varied little to that point: river on the right, fungus-covered trees on the left, the hard-packed turf of the path between. Patches of berry-filled brambles sometimes grow dense enough to block direct view into the woods, especially at the eye level of the three diminutive travelers. The Zoogs following them—and Jake is convinced they are there—continue to stay completely out of sight.

At times, catching random movements out of the corner of his eye, he stops to stare into the trees, but nothing is ever there. During these pauses, the ever-present need to locate the odor of the bird-thing forces him to try, but the attempts are half-hearted. Still, moist air conspires with the clouds to lock the scents of Zoogs, humans, and cats into place. The occasional bird—live bird—is detected, but not the one associated with that tickle in his nose.

Eventually, the clouds thin, revealing splashes of cheerful blue betwixt them. With the sun getting a chance to show its face at times, the cool, dreary morning warms up nicely. Too nicely.

Thirsty, Jake spots a relatively shallow section of the bank. Making his way down to the river's edge, a sniff convinces him that the water is okay to drink. If needed. But something about it makes him hesitate. It's almost as if he knows he shouldn't.

"Jake," calls out Algernon before he can take an experimental lap. "Only drink from the river when you have no other choice."

Bounding back to them, he asks, "Is there a stream around here?"

"Not a stream. But there is water not far from here."

Resuming their journey, the cat stops periodically to examine the surroundings. Finally satisfied, he bobs his head to the left and heads into the brambles. As low as the trio are, it's not too difficult to push through. Jake can see signs of a path having been there, but long years of neglect had allowed the overgrowth to mask it. An impression in a spot of bare ground appears to be the print of a shoe, and a sniff confirms it, but that remnant of humanity is old.

Once through the choking vines, it's not far into the trees when they reach a small, cleared space. Centered within that area is a pile of stones with metal and wood attached. A moist whiff of water hangs in the air.

"This well was built by people," says Algernon. "Few know of it."

"Well?" asks Jake.

"Water," says Sandy. "A hole with water at the bottom."

Capped with stone, access to it doesn't seem possible. Jake walks completely around it to be sure, and spots nothing, but does pick up a newer odor. A cat, maybe? One visited not long ago, on a route through the trees rather than from the trail.

"How do we get to the water?" he asks.

"It can be pumped up," says Algernon. "When this piece of wood, this pedal, is stepped on repeatedly, water comes up from below and out of that spout."

Jake accepts the explanation, uncertain of the processes involved. In his own home, the kitchen sink seems to operate in a more magical and mysterious way: Touches of the silver handle are enough to start and stop the flow.

"Any human, even a child, has enough weight and strength to operate it," continues Algernon. "Two cats cannot make it work, but three can."

"Which means that we can," says Sandy.

"Or, with Jake, perhaps just two. The most difficult part will be getting it moving. All three of us will be needed for that."

Jake looks at the wood, but full comprehension eludes him.

"What do I do?" he asks.

With the cat directing, they try different configurations around the wooden pedal before settling on one that gives Jake the best chance to take advantage of his mass without interfering with the efforts of the other two.

"We need to remove our weight when it's all the way down," Algernon reminds them.

Despite evidence that someone had been by recently to use it, the mechanism is stubborn. Applying their combined weight to the pedal, they do push it down. A wheel connected to the pedal via a metal bar turns slowly, reluctantly. A chorus of squeaking rewards their efforts, but all three miss the mark with their timing. Sandy and Algernon stop too soon, Jake too late. The pedal rises, then freezes. Having seen the motion of the wheel, Jake at least understands the linkage between it and the pedal. The exact mechanics are far from being grasped, but a light glows a little more brightly in his mind.

"I believe I know what the issue is," says Algernon. "The pedal was not at its full height." Springing over to the wheel, he places one front paw on a roughly horizontal spoke, then the other, and tries to pull down. "The wheel needs to turn more. That will raise the pedal up."

Realizing that he's needed, and that Sandy is too small to help, Jake joins the cat. Standing side by side, they both pull. It resists at first, then, under the might of four paws, moves. Loud creaking fades as the spoke rotates down. When nearly vertical, Algernon jumps away. His neck wavers back and forth as he studies the pedal and wheel.

"Jake. Do the same thing with the next spoke."

Extending himself, he latches on the bar above him and pulls. A steady effort brings it down, down, …

"Stop," says Algernon. "That should be enough."

Releasing his grip and returning to the pedal, Jake can tell there's a difference with it, noticeably higher than when they had first arrived.

All three resituate themselves.

"Ready?" asks Algernon. "Remember to take your weight off when the pedal is at the bottom, and let it rise up to this height before pressing down again."

For Jake, the instructions make sense, though he looks to Sandy for guidance.

"We'll follow your lead," she says, and Jake barks agreement.

"Now," says Algernon.

All three apply their weight.

The pedal sinks.

With the rust having been loosened, the wheel does turn more easily this time, though still with plenty of complaints. At the low point, they move off. Inertia takes over, keeping the heavy wheel rotating. The pedal rises…far enough. Barely, but enough.

"Again," commands Algernon.

There's less noise on second cycle.

On the third, Jake has the rhythm and he no longer needs to watch the cat. With momentum having been built up and the worst of the rust flaked away, it's much easier to keep it going. And, as far as Jake is concerned, it's fun. It's so entertaining, in fact, that he's startled when a stream of water erupts from the spout. An ugly color to begin, it runs clear after a short while.

"You go first, Sandy," says Algernon. "Jake, stay here with me."

Placing herself under the flow, she tries to drink—and does—but gets soaked. Having gotten enough, she returns to her spot at the pedal.

"I'll go next," says the cat.

Instead of staying low and trying to catch water near the ground, he stands on rear legs and steadies himself against the spout with the front. Stretching his neck, he laps from the outflow at the source. Some drops splash onto his face, but he winds up with only wet paws.

"Sandy and I will try to keep this going," says Algernon, resuming his position. "But I don't think we can for very long. What you need to do is press down, then jump over for a drink, then come back and help us, then go back. Back and forth. Understand?"

Jake does.

And what he comes to understand better is that this set of actions—press down, leap over, drink, leap back—is more fun than repeating the press and pause had been. Unable to keep them contained, enthusiastic barks escape and echo through the trees. His joy infectious, Sandy wags her approval and joins in.

Then he sees it: a flash of brown. There, then gone.

63

What?

Having had plenty enough of the water, he stops and stares at the spot that had, for an eyeblink, contained the head, chest, and arms of a rat-like creature with oversized ears. Eyes flared, it had looked terrified.

"Did you see a Zoog?" asks Algernon, scanning the area.

"I saw something."

"Your excitement must have alarmed them. There are dogs here, but they stay with the humans in the towns. Or on farms. We know that you were simply enjoying yourself, but that was a novel experience for them. Shocking, perhaps."

Addressing the deep woods, Algernon shouts a few, shrill syllables.

"What did you say?" asks Sandy. "I thought there would be a single language here. We can communicate with you and the priest. Even the vulture."

"I apologized for our outburst."

Her head tilts. When she looks at Jake, he shrugs.

"That didn't sound like an apology," she says.

"Because cats and dogs and humans share the waking world, that common thread binds our minds together, making communication easy. Zoogs are different, and their language is very different. Alien. Their tribal culture can be violent, and the language reflects that."

Sandy scowls, but Jake accepts that he has a lot to learn about this new, foreign place.

"If we're done here, we should be on our way," suggests the cat.

When the two dogs nod assent, they start off.

"Will there be many wells along the way?" asks Jake.

"They are more common to the east, but this is the only one we needed to make use of. It is quite a distance to the next stream. I strongly prefer to not drink from the river. Especially the farther we go."

"Why?"

"As I said before, we will be passing towns. And where there are too many humans gathered together, even here, in dream, there is a disruption in the natural order of things."

The meaning of those words is lost on Jake, but Sandy seems to understand.

"That is a tactful way of putting it," she says. "And I can't dispute that. But why haven't we seen any?"

"For whatever reason, few come here."

"Along this path, you mean?"

"This entire world. In recent times, there has been a dramatic fall in the number who descend the steps from the Cavern of Flame. This place has always had its own human society created from the energy of the collective subconscious, and a certain inertia guarantees its continued existence. But some aspect of the waking world is erasing the need for humans to explore their dreams."

Sandy only grunts in response.

A steady pace brings a welcome change of scene. Although the trees across the river had looked much the same as they had the entire way so far, the ones on this bank change. Great, drooping fronds of willows replace the broad-leafed varieties they had walked beside and beneath. Thickly clustered for a while, the willows thin out—subtly, then substantially. Then the trees are gone altogether, succeeded by meadows of clover.

Hills and valleys come and go under their paws, introducing elevation changes that break up the monotonous flatness. Fields of wheat appear, along with farmhouses, offering proof of human habitation. Sheep and goats graze, watched over by their herders. Parallel to their trail, a much larger dirt road comes into view. Carts, some empty but many filled with wares, roll along on it intermittently, drawn by sturdy horses or donkeys.

In short, the world becomes much more interesting for Jake: new sights, sounds, smells… Oh, the smells! All of those people and animals and plants that he sees have a matching odor. A strongly pungent flower makes him suddenly realize that the ever-present Zoog-smell is gone. Excitedly assuming that he'll be able to sniff out the badness that he needs to track, he inhales.

And sifts through the array of odors.

And does not find it.

A second effort again comes up empty. Despite the assurance from the cat, Jake can't help but believe that another vulture trip will be needed. The replay of that horrifying dive makes his stomach flip.

"Coming?" asks a voice.

He had been close to Sandy and Algernon, but now they're far ahead, stopped, looking back.

"Is something wrong?" asks Sandy.

"Oh. Umm. No."

Sauntering up to them, he wonders if he should broach the subject. Algernon hasn't mentioned it yet. Will he be soon asked to get another fix on the smell, then be forced to admit that he can't. Should he lie?

"Sorry," he offers. "I was just thinking." Which is not a lie.

The anxiety remains, however.

Taking breaks occasionally, they walk through the afternoon. Off in the distance, the many terraces of a town come into view, covering a hillside all the way down to the river's edge. With the red-brown stones polished as they are, the structures gleam in the sunlight.

"That is Kiran," says Algernon, nodding toward the town. "We will stay there tonight."

"Can we get some water soon?" asks Jake. Their drink from the well was far behind them.

"We have a bit further to go, but yes. We can eat and drink before getting to the town."

As they continue, Jake's thirst grows and he is tempted more and more to ask Algernon exactly what "a bit further" means to a cat, but holds his tongue. Finally, the sun having lowered greatly, the stone walls of Kiran no longer far off at all, their path is interrupted by a bridge. As Jake hopes, a stream flows beneath it.

Once across, they veer off the route, upstream, through a grassy patch that slopes gently down to meet the water. The cool liquid soothes his parched throat. Refreshed, he recalls the faint barks he's heard during the recent miles, and wistfully wonders if any dogs are nearby.

"What's your name?"

Bewildered by the strange voice, Jake turns to see a medium-sized dog, with the distribution of white, black, and brown across the fur almost identical to his own. Head tilted, tail whipping with sharp enthusiasm, he's definitely not a threat.

"I'm Jake."

"What's your name?" asks the new dog again.

"I told you. It's Jake. What's yours?"

"Want to play?" The wags coming even faster, his front dipping low, rear shooting high.

"Go home," growls Sandy.

With a happy "Home" bark, the unnamed dog takes off, splashing upstream for a short way before dashing up a bank.

"What was wrong with him?" asks Jake.

"The dogs here are…different," frowns Sandy. "For some reason."

"Deaf?"

"No. More like…" She searches for a word. "Stupid."

"Why?"

"The living things in this world that have an equivalent in the waking one are projections of what the mass subconsciousness expects them to be," explains Algernon. "Idealized."

"And the ideal dog is happy and stupid?" asks Sandy, ire up.

"I am only describing the way of things," remarks Algernon.

For Jake, the topic hits uncomfortably close to home.

"What about cats?" he asks with a glare.

Algernon stiffens.

"Yes," chimes in Sandy. "Answer Jake's question. What about cats?"

"Originally, the cats here were no better," replies Algernon. "But that mistake was corrected long, long ago."

"Corrected?" asks Sandy. "How?"

Tail flicking madly, the cat says nothing.

"HOW?"

"Every single one of those mockeries was tracked down and eliminated," says Algernon pointedly. "A great effort was then made to ensure that every cat in the waking world could find the entrance to this place. The dream-selves of waking cats supplanted the sham versions that were here."

It's hard for Jake to believe what he's hearing, but his friend's unmoving tail verifies it.

"You went to war against your own?" she asks.

The cat takes a deep breath and releases it.

"It was deemed to be necessary," he says with a shrug.

"We're alone here, Jake," murmurs Sandy.

On the trail nothing is said. Jake is dumbfounded. Algernon's admission sits amid his thoughts, a singularly unpleasant weight. Unaware of the formal label of *genocide*, that leaden nugget rolls and clanks around maddeningly in the jar of his brain. Sandy had said at the start of their journey that she trusted no cats, and this astonishing disclosure seems to be an excellent reason to reinforce that stance.

But the way that dog had acted had been just as disheartening. On any other day, when not on a quest with Sandy and Algernon, Jake would have been eager to run and play. The thing had looked like a real dog, but had acted like one in only the most superficial manner. Algernon had used the word sham, and it is an awful truth. The dogs here are innocent and playful, but cannot be considered real. Though animated and full of energy, Jake knows that some spark, or energy, is missing. The abstract notion of *soul* is what he zeroes in on, but that particular word is also missing from his education.

There's so much percolating within Jake's mind that he wants to discuss with Sandy, but she's tight-jawed, continuing to fume. The presence of the cat would be a hindrance anyway.

With the red-brown walls of the town close by, Algernon stops and motions toward an overgrown field.

"Dinner," is all he says before disappearing into the undergrowth.

Sandy stares at the spot he stepped into, and a moment later a rabbit hops out. Oddly colored, it's the same grey as Algernon, including the splash of white. Large eyes sweep over the dogs before it takes a few hops and settles down to nibble some clover, the two predators in its blind spot.

"Sit down," whispers Sandy. "This one is mine."

Sneaking up directly behind it, she makes progress a bit at a time. There's a leap and a chomp. The rabbit, bigger than Sandy, nearly flings her off. The muscled rear legs dig in and try to hop with the added weight, but the diminutive dog stays locked onto the neck.

The pair twist and spin in place.

Dust flies.

There's a final spasm from the rabbit, then all is still.

Panting, Sandy stands. With a hungry smile, Jake bounds over to her and they begin to rip the thing apart. But Sandy doesn't stop with simply opening the carcass for easier access. She pulls off each limb and completely eviscerates it. Only when the rabbit is reduced to a disordered collection of parts do they eat their fill.

Taken aback by the ferocity of his little friend, Jake gives her first choice of mouthfuls and all the room she wants.

After Sandy takes a quick dip in the river to wash off the worst of the dirt and blood, the dogs meet up with Algernon.

Glancing at the messy remains and grey fur, the cat raises its eyebrows.

"I was going to ask if you enjoyed your meal," he says, squinting at Sandy. "But I can see that I don't need to."

He turns his back on them and heads toward the town.

Watching the cat, Sandy growls something that Jake doesn't catch.

"Let's go," she adds more loudly.

While the trail proper hugs the river below the lowest reaches of Kiran, a branch to the left leads up a gentle hillside to the main gate. The road that they had seen is very close now, running through that gate. And though Algernon had said that they would stay in the town, he leads them past that spur. It's only further on, where the towering walls nearly kiss the river, when he again veers off the path.

Hidden behind foliage on the left, the base of the wall has four semicircular arches, spaced evenly apart. It's through the first of those openings that the cat crawls. Sandy is able to get through easily, but Jake struggles to squeeze through. Tilting onto his side, he claws his way in.

Darkness greets his eyes, though not a total blackness. The final remnants of the day filter through holes in the ceiling high above, as well as the ones at ground level. Though it gives the illusion of being a cave, the smooth, flat walls around them imply that they're in a man-made room. A large pool of water occupies most of it, with a statue of a man seated in a throne at its westernmost edge. Sculpted of a white stone, there are golden accents that glint even in the fading light.

Stuffy and humid, water drips from high above, plinking and plunking into the pool.

"Do not drink this water," cautions Algernon, his words an echoing susurrus in the chamber. "This is a sacred place. A shrine to the river."

Opposite the statue, there is an opening in the wall with steps leading upward. An alcove to the right of it has a series of shelves, hewn from the rock and lined with ornamented containers filled with varieties of incense. Despite the lids, the aromas wafting from there are far too intense for Jake. His nose engulfed, he sneezes. Twice.

"That is less than sacred," frowns Algernon.

"Sorry", apologizes Jake. "Too many flowers here."

"Not for me," announces Sandy, spinning down onto the floor. "I'll sleep here."

Sampling the air as he goes, Jake gets as far away as he can, plopping down behind the statue. Before his lids shut, he watches the cat lie down on the floor next to the hole through which they entered.

What?

Jake wakes up, looks, listens…

Nothing.

It's obviously later, obviously nighttime. Infinitesimal flecks of starlight can be seen through the openings in the ceiling, grains of salt against the blackness. And some amount of moonlight leaks in through the openings in the base of the wall facing the river, enough for him to be able to tell that the shape of Algernon is right where he had last been.

But there is also a glow.

Standing, creeping around the statue, his eyes pick up a shape. Two shapes. Ephemeral, made of cloud-stuff, they hover above the water: a man, bearded and muscular, and a woman, slight of build, yet giving an impression of tremendous power. Both naked, they kneel, facing each other. Their lips move in turns, as if having a conversation, but all that Jake can hear is the dripping of droplets into the pool.

The man seems to ask a question. The woman points a ghostly finger at Jake. The man turns to Jake, studies him, looking up and down. Then, Jake feels as if he's being examined—almost like being at the V.E.T. The people there are always nice to him, but the cries and odors of terror are too much for any dog to completely ignore. Here, now, there's merely a faint pressure on his head, in his chest. Although bizarre, the experience isn't the least bit alarming.

Finished, the man of fog smiles at the bemused dog. He mouths a single, silent word.

Rest.

Is it a suggestion or a command? Jake flumps down. Sleep returns.

In the morning, he wakes to a symphony of drips into the pool, a far more constant melody than the staccato notes from the night before. Sure enough, right next to one of the arched openings, it's easy to hear the rain outside.

"I've been awake for a while," says Algernon. "The rain has slowed greatly and will stop soon."

"Did you see or hear anything weird during the night?" asks Jake, the memory of his dream-within-a-dream incomplete.

"In what way?"

Jake shakes his head, trying to get the pieces to stick together. But they only bounce apart.

"I don't know," he sighs.

"I saw nothing out of the ordinary last night." With a bob of his head toward Sandy, he adds, "Her legs are doing the most work of the three of us. We can allow her some extra rest before getting underway again."

Jake nods agreement and sits down. An uncomfortable silence ensues. Watching the cat, unable to dispel yesterday's shocking revelations, words tumble from Jake's mouth before he realizes he's speaking them.

"Dogs are different from cats, aren't they?"

Feline eyes narrow.

"Oh, Jake. You are a treasure." His whiskers twitch. "I only laugh with delight. You are a delightful soul. And yes: Dogs and cats are indeed different. Please, have a drink from the pool if you are thirsty."

"Really?"

"Yes."

"I thought," said Sandy, coming into view, "you told us last night to not do that."

"I did," replied Algernon. "But that was before judgement was passed. Having been deemed worthy, you may both partake."

"We were judged? By whom? When did that happen?"

"I can only say that, had there been an issue, we would not have been permitted to stay."

With a mutual shrug, the two dogs cautiously lap from the pool. Clean, but with a tingly effervescence, it provides Jake with a burst of energy to erase the laziness of the night.

Squirming back through the hole, the three emerge into a damp world. As Algernon had predicted, the rain lightens to a drizzle as they go. Past the town, evidence of man's attempts to tame the wilderness vanish. There are no farms to the east of the city, only the random array that nature creates: scrub and brush, meadows of grasses or wildflowers, stands of trees that thicken into forest. In other words, it's a wonderful place for them to find breakfast. After the pause to hunt and eat, the drizzle is gone, some brightening of the sky hinting that the day will eventually dry.

And it does. They amble onward, the path taking them straight east over rolling hills, the river on their right. The road that had been accompanying them was visible as it exited the gates on the eastern side of Kiran, but now it bends northward. Soon, the dense trees near the river conceal their view of it.

That day, water isn't a problem. They come across streams more often than needed, all having bridges, either of stone or wood. Algernon is in no especial hurry, and he has them take frequent rest breaks. Jake never seems to get physically tired from the endless marching, but he notices a mental sluggishness if they go too long between sit-downs. Sandy seems to have recovered from her anger of the previous day, and all chat in a friendly manner, but only about what is around them. Or the weather. Or the rodents in the area. Nothing controversial.

Mid-afternoon, the sun does break through the clouds and its rays call attention to what Algernon indicates is their destination for this day: Thran. The golden tips of its many spires, set atop glistening, white towers periodically come into view as they crest a hill, only to be hidden again upon descending into the next vale. Tall, thin houses are how Sandy explains the unique collection of buildings to Jake.

Closer to the town the land flattens, becoming tame, treeless fields once again. With nothing to obscure them, those spokes gleam brilliantly against the blue sky. So dazzling are they that it's difficult to look directly at them for any length of time. The bottoms are rooted behind walls that are just as spectacular: perfectly seamless, blindingly white in the sun, they rise higher than any tree in their awake neighborhood.

People can be seen sporadically, far off, guiding oxen as they plow, or watching over sheep. When the first finally appear on the trail, Jake is tempted to run up to greet them. Two women, one younger, one older, burdened with packages, slowly trundle toward them. But a thought tickles his brain, a sobering one, stopping him in his tracks. His tail stops.

Do they expect me to be happy and stupid?

"When possible, we should not be seen," recommends Algernon, eying the women.

Happy and stupid?

"Jake," says Sandy when he fails to move. "Let's go."

He sullenly nods and follows.

From behind a thicket of trees, they watch the pair go by. The older one reminds Jake of Linda, in a vague way. He wants a pat on the head and a belly rub so much that he could fairly scream. But he feels—he knows—that it's a bad idea.

"You two should eat now, while no one else is around," says the cat. "I'll have plenty of choice morsels in the city. You'll likely prefer the pickings out here. I'll keep a lookout if you want to chase something down."

In no mood to eat, much less run, Jake hangs his head and shakes it.

"We can do this quickly," says Sandy.

From beneath the bush next to them, an ordinary brown cottontail climbs up from its burrow. She pounces and subdues it, but can't kill it. When Jake also gets hold, a sharp tug cracks its neck. He gulps down his portion, brooding over the two women. And beyond them, all of the people in this world. And how they think of him.

Happy and stupid.
Happy.
And.
Stupid.

Staying off the path, they make their way toward the city. Where the southernmost tip of Thran touches the water, ships are moored along numerous docks that jut into the river. That gate is heavily guarded, however. Fierce-looking sentries armed with swords stop and quiz all who wish to enter. There are other, smaller entry points, but it hardly seems any easier to get through one of those, each also manned.

The sun low, they steal through the long shadows toward a less-popular entrance and hunker down behind a clump of weeds.

"We're going in that one," says Algernon.

To Jake, it's the worst possible option.

"That one? It has a dog! And it looks mean."

Mean is an understatement. Teeth bared and growling almost continuously when anyone nears, it is the stereotypical guard dog, the embodiment of fierce, unblinking, loyal protection.

"That dog," says Algernon, "is exactly why." Leaning back, he then yowls something incomprehensible, but very cat-like.

That catches the attention of the dog. Searching intently, it tries to find the source.

"What was that?" asks Sandy.

"A call for help. Aid, I should say."

"From?"

"Them."

As if by magic, felines materialize from the surrounding grasses. Of every color and style, they approach and study the dogs, most wrinkling their noses. One by one, they settle in, forming a semicircle in front of Algernon, and wait.

"We welcome you," says Algernon to the assemblage, over a dozen strong.

"You come with two dogs?" snarls a female black cat. "The protocols have been shat upon."

"This is an unusual situation."

"A justification is required," she insists.

"I invoke the equal-paws exemption for these two."

"Under whose authority?"

When Algernon screeches a single syllable, the effect on the cats is unmistakable. All come to stiff attention, eyes on him.

"I am Ariadne," says the black cat. "I apologize for my suspicion."

"There is no need to apologize. Suspicion in such circumstances is normal. As I stated, this is unusual."

Ariadne glances at the dogs.

"Indeed," she says. "What needs to be done?"

"First, a diversion in order to get these two through that entrance."

Ariadne looks to her left. Three cats break off from that end of the line and slink away.

"They will wait for your signal. What else?"

"A place to spend the night. Also, in the morning we will need access to the highest tower in the south or east of—"

Highest? Tomorrow?

The need to go up high again had been mentioned, and known, to Jake, but without the timing of it defined to that point. With the immediacy of *tomorrow* being presented so suddenly, his fear crystallizes. That horrible memory of flight makes his heart skip a beat.

Wait. Not a vulture.

He recalls the blazing towers from this afternoon, now only barely visible. Sandy's description of them, the knowledge that his paws would not be floating in the sky, brings a measure of calm. But a threatening bark from the guard dog—a closer and more visceral danger—is what snaps him out of his brooding.

"—who can be trusted," finishes Algernon.

"Sleeping arrangements will be easy," says Ariadne. "Access to a tower will also not be an issue. For the final request, I'll need to ask around."

"Do so. You are aware of the import."

"I am."

"Good. We will meet you inside."

The cats break rank.

"Sandy. Jake. We'll have an opportunity shortly. Pay attention to the man. Stay behind him and do not allow him to see you. Once inside, listen to Ariadne."

"We can trust her?" asks Sandy.

"She has been tasked with keeping the two of you safe. Your fates are all joined."

Notwithstanding the stealthy efforts of the dogs and cats, the guard dog seems to sense their movements. Long, fruitless minutes are spent scanning the surroundings. Then, with a satisfied snort, it relaxes.

"Now," hisses Algernon into the dusk.

A wave of field mice floods in. The man swats at them with his sword, annoyed and perplexed. The dog reacts like any dog would.

"Mouse!" it barks, over and over, delirious with excitement. Biting at a few, it mainly bats at them with its paws. But it stays at its post.

Then the cats make their presence known. They sweep in alternately, coming closer to the dog with each pass. The guard tries to chase them away, but the crafty felines have the reach of his weapon measured.

The activity is too much for the dog. Barking maniacally, it tears after a cat. All three then work together, leading it away. Focused on the mayhem, the man takes a step. And another. It's a small gap, but enough.

Waiting for that moment, Algernon leads them in a curving route, taking advantage of shrubs and bushes to get directly behind the man before closing the distance. The area nearest the entrance is a challenge, bare of all vegetation due the passage of uncounted feet.

They pause—too long—at the edge of that clearing before making the dash. With the trio most of the way to their destination, the guard's patience runs out.

"REX! Get back here!"

Jake can see the man's attention is solely on the dog. With not that far to go, and kicking their speed up a notch, he feels that they can make it.

But the dog, turning to look at his master, spots the intruders. "Hey!" it barks. "Strange dogs!" Racing back, the cats are forgotten.

Algernon gets through.

Then Sandy.

"Strange dogs! Hey!"

Every bark sends a nervous jitter through Jake. The dog has been announcing the problem; the man only need turn a little. But he never does.

And Jake is in!

He wants to keep running, but Ariadne is there, blocking and guiding him to the base of the wall they had just passed through, not far at all from the opening. Expecting to be attacked, he turns and makes ready.

Only the dog's head and upper body flash into view before it's rudely pulled back. There's a yelp.

From their vantage, the legs and feet of the guard become visible as he resumes his post. And all of the protesting whines of "Strange dogs" go ignored.

The full day of travel, topped off with a rush of adrenaline at the end, is more than enough to exhaust Jake. Able to spend the night on a soft pile of hay, and with no distracting dreams, he wakens reenergized.

"I needed that," says Sandy, echoing his thoughts.

They both stretch and look around. There had been only the faintest glimmers of evening light when led to this underground room. Now, they can make out some details. The presence of a door, slightly ajar, is the only item that qualifies the space as a room. The ceiling is not a typical one, being lined with the parallel timbers of floor joists. And it's so low here that only a small child would be able to stand up straight.

The odors of humanity are all around, strong, but not overpowering. And cats have visited, too. No dogs, though.

When the door swings inward, Algernon enters, followed by three more cats, each with a dead chipmunk.

"Good morning," says Algernon. "Here is your breakfast. Freshly killed."

Despite the taste reminding Jake of squirrel, the meal is still a satisfying start to the day. He has two, plus a little of Sandy's that she doesn't finish.

"I'm going up high today?" he asks after the last mouthful. "In a tower?"

"You are. And it is good that you've eaten that much. You'll need the energy to climb many, many steps."

Snaking their way through alleys, at times even threading their way between legs, Algernon leads them through a city that is beginning to stir. The rising sun, not yet high enough to make it over the walls, only illumines the golden tips of the spires. Everything glows in that yellow-tinged light.

Not far from the southern gate, a sign labels an inn as being *The Broken Goat*. Jake can't read the words, but he does take note of a picture of a goat, one curving horn whole, the other only half-length and splintered.

In a small yard near the door is Ariadne.

"The young, bearded man seated at the window," she says, nodding toward him. "He arrived two days ago, from Celephais. He may appear to be too young, but his dreams have taken him far. He is the best option at this point in time."

"How many others are inside?" asks Algernon.

"Only the innkeepers are downstairs. An older man and woman. They will not interfere."

"And the tower?"

"Arrangements have been made."

"Good. Stand guard. This should not take too long." He instructs the dogs, "Come in with me and say nothing at all unless I tell you."

At the door, Algernon scratches the wood and meows in an especially long, drawn out manner. It opens, and a weathered, but sturdy, man looks down.

"Would you like some milk?" he asks. When Algernon doesn't react, he follows with, "Or would you like to come in?" When the second query is answered with a short mew, he steps aside.

The cat darts in, but the door starts to close before the dogs can enter.

Through the crack, Jake sees the cat stop and explain, "Mraow."

"The dogs, too?"

Algernon stares up and tilts his head, which is apparently enough for the man.

"Okay," he says. The door opens wide. "I believe the gods can happily take my soul, for now I have seen everything." All three animals inside, he shuts the door and asks Algernon, "Do you need anything else?"

"I suspect that they're here to see me," says the younger man seated at the window. "At least, the cat is."

With a shrug, the older man departs.

"I have to agree with Howard," continues the young man as the trio take a seat on the floor in front of him. "This particular sight is nothing I would have ever dreamt of adding to my list of the yet-unseen."

To Jake, the voice is pleasant, tinged with kindness, and his scent is remarkably comforting.

"There is a reason for this irregularity," begins the cat. "My name is Algernon, and I have been informed that you can be trusted."

"I'm Ben. Trust is a difficult currency, but I believe that my explorations and reputation have allowed me to establish a line of credit among cats. Ariadne and I have friends in common. Based on that, she may be able to vouch for me."

"She has. But I need to be sure. Are you aware of the treaty of Hrruz?"

"I am. I can quote you the compromise between Ophelia and King Marquand, if you'd like."

"Not necessary. Can you describe the land that the eighth gate of Ilarnek opens upon?"

Ben's eyes sparkle as he grins.

"I wish I could," he says, "but Ilarnek has only seven gates."

"Good. And have you been briefed on the Klopkt edict and its implications?"

"I know of it," he replies with a frown, "but I have to admit not knowing the details."

Algernon's whiskers droop.

"I see."

"But I have been beneath fabled Irem, down to the fifth level. With Theodore, whom Ariadne knows. Our expedition was cut short when we were detected by—"

"Yes," interjects the cat. More calmly, he adds, "They-who-watch-from-above."

"Exactly," says Ben, glancing upward.

Algernon pauses a long while before speaking again.

"The fifth, you say?" he asks. "What is the color of the protective sigil on the floor?"

"Silver. Etched into blackest obsidian."

Eyes shut tightly, tail thrashing, the cat says nothing—although, at times, his mouth forms unvoiced words. Finally, his eyes open.

"This is a difficult decision, but extraordinary times require extraordinary measures. Jake, please explain to the best of your ability what we are doing."

Hearing the dog's name is enough to raise Ben's eyebrows, but when Jake begins to speak, he stares in fascination.

"I don't know where it came from, but I found a bad thing in the park. Not here. It was in my park when I'm awake. It was there, then it wasn't. Then it came back and Sandy sent it into this dream place. We're trying to find it. I can smell it but I need to be up high."

The man's head slowly shakes back and forth

"What?" he asks, blinking.

"And I don't want to take another vulture trip," adds Jake.

Too many words try to leap out of Ben's mouth at the same time.

"That's the first—How did—I've—"

Hesitant, smiling, he reaches out to the dog.

Overjoyed, tail whipping madly, Jake scoots closer and lowers his head. Sandy does the same.

"This," says Algernon, "is the secret with which you are being entrusted. Jake and Sandy are the first dogs to enter this realm from the waking world."

"This is a fabulous secret," says Ben, petting both. "And the bad thing you're trying to find?"

"We're not entirely sure what it is," says the cat. "I have a suspicion, but will not voice it."

86

"And what do you need me for?"

"The towers of Thran provide an excellent opportunity for Jake to scent out this thing. Get a bearing. But we know that the windows at the top are set too high off the floor for him. We need you to lift him up."

"I've never been in any of the towers."

"Few humans have," says Algernon. "The entrances are disguised, and there are certain difficulties associated with them."

"Guards? There are plenty enough of those in Thran."

"No."

"Locks?"

"Sometimes."

"What then?"

Algernon hesitates.

"There are curses," he says. "They do not affect cats, only humans."

"What about dogs?" asks Sandy.

"I cannot say. Although, with the intent to keep humans out, it seems extremely unlikely that dogs are affected."

"The specific one to be climbed," says Ben, eyes no longer as lively as they had been. "What is the curse?"

"Again, we have not been able to determine that. We only know that one man who was within the tower emerged with no visible harm."

"And so, it is not instantly lethal."

"Correct. Or obviously damaging."

"Are you sure that Ben is needed?" asks Sandy.

"We are. The windows are narrow, set at the height of a man's shoulders. Jake can jump that high but he will need help to work his nose out far enough to get a scent."

Those words are apparently enough for the man to decide.

"Okay," he says, eyes sparkling once again. "You have a job to do, and I have an interest in meeting more like these two in this world." He ruffles both dogs' fur at the same time, one with each hand. "Let's be off before I change my mind!"

Lead by Ariadne, the group leave the inn. The city is bustling already, the vendors set up in the marketplace, some loudly hawking their wares. The cats who had brought breakfast for the dogs stay ahead, scouting, or guarding, or doing whatever it is that cats on the prowl do.

In one crowded area, when Sandy is kicked and nearly stepped on, Ben snatches her up. She wags her approval, though manages to bang into his jaw when she shakes her head. He rubs his face then gives Sandy a pat as she lays her head on his shoulder.

Eventually, they come to an opening at the base of a tower. Craning his neck back, Jake can see the tip a daunting distance above, a golden jewel set against velvet blue.

Through the archway, stairs lead down. But, instead of getting darker as they descend, it's just the opposite. At the bottom, a turn of the corner reveals an open doorway with warm light pouring out. The door itself is made of stout timbers, banded with metal and set on sturdy hinges. Outside of that opening sits a pair of cats.

"This is the entrance," says Ariadne. "The light you see is actually sunlight reflected down the length of the spiraling stairs."

She walks over the threshold, then back out. "As you can see, nothing happened to me. Jake, would you like to try?"

"I'll do it," volunteers Sandy.

When Ben sets her down, she goes straight in. After a short wait, sniffing and listening, she returns.

"No difference that I can feel," reports Sandy.

All eyes fall on Ben.

"What might happen?" he asks.

Ariadne hangs her head and paws at the stone floor.

"Tell him," says Algernon.

"In the tower abutting the north gate, the light is so bright that it blinds the moment that the door is opened. For the one next to the Temple of the Outer Gods, men have been seen to die of fright. Another curse induces ringing in the ears so unrelenting that it causes insanity. And in the very highest tower in the heart of the city, men vanish as soon as they set foot inside, never to be seen again. I can go on, if you like."

"I get the idea," says Ben with a grim smile. "But none of those apply here, correct?"

"We assume so. All of the curses seem to be unique. We only recently solved the problem of opening this door. To this point, one man has been observed exiting. He sealed it immediately and refused to share any details of his experience or tell us how to gain entrance."

"But seemed to be otherwise unharmed?"

Ariadne nods.

"An intriguing curse, to be sure."

"Now is the time to go, or not," prods Algernon.

There is a long pause, but Ben finally steps through the doorway.

"Nothing so far," he says.

"Perhaps the curse only becomes evident at the top," suggests Algernon.

"I suppose I'll find out. Are you ready, Jake?"

Walking in, Jake feels nothing except for the stone beneath his paws.

"I guess we should go," he says, starting up the curving set. Set at a standard height, the steps won't be a difficult effort, at least to begin. He wonders how many times he'll wind around and around.

With the dog having a comfortable lead, Ben sets foot on the first step.

"Oh." A tiny utterance, it nevertheless overflows with something. Pleasure?

Jake stops and looks back.

"What?" asks Sandy from below.

"I know," replies Ben, voice hollow. "I know."

"What do you know?"

But Ben says nothing else and takes another step. Then a third.

Jake hasn't known the man long, but the dullness of his eyes gives the impression that he's only partially conscious. Not asleep, but deep in thought? Maybe.

The winding staircase is narrow, but there is enough room for Jake to squeeze past his legs and get behind him. But what if Ben were to fall? Too large for Jake to catch or help, they would probably both be hurt.

Better to stay in front.

With the befogged man advancing at a steady pace, Jake heads up.

Four steps, pause, look back.

Four steps, pause, look back.

There are no floors. Or platforms. Only stairs.

Endlessly upward, Jake climbs with Ben in tow. At regular intervals—though his canine brain hasn't yet learned to count that high—a slit is cut into the stone, letting in a refreshing breeze. Algernon had said the windows at the top would be barely wide enough for Jake to wriggle through; these match that design. A series of mirrors and lenses, mounted high on the outer wall, provides the illumination, passing the rays downward in an uninterrupted chain.

Though Jake rests frequently, and his legs are weary despite of it, the man behind him never does. Eyes glazed, Ben steps mechanically. Though breathing heavily from the exertion, he seems unwilling to stop or even slow.

Four steps, pause, look back.

Four steps, pause, look back.

They keep going. And going.

At last, there is an end.

Seeing a flat spot ahead, Jake forces himself to bound up the last, curved stretch. At the top is a circular room, four slits for windows set at the points of a compass. And, as he had been told, they look to be inches above the reach of his front paws were he to stand on his rear ones.

Though there are no more stairs, his muscles spasm, wanting to keep climbing. But he forces himself to sit down, away from the floor opening.

Ben's head appears. Torso. Legs.

And he's up.

Then down, collapsing on the floor. It's a slow, controlled fall, but it's clear that the man is spent. Flat on the floor, taking deep breaths, he rubs his legs. Whatever spell or curse he was under seems to be gone.

"Are you alright?" asks Jake quietly.

"I am," replies Ben. "But exhausted. I need to rest."

"Sure."

But the silence of their rest lasts only a short time. The man begins to chuckle, then laugh. Concerned at first, Jake can hear joy in the outburst. He wags his tail, adding in howls of his own.

As the laughter dies away, Ben sits up and looks directly into the dog's eyes.

"I know," he says, then adds with a grin, "Everything."

"What do you mean?"

"Everything! Every detail of this world was revealed to me on the way up. With each step I learned more and more. I wasn't being forced to keep going. Rather, it was so intoxicating that I couldn't help myself." He sighs, and Jake can hear it oozing with the contentment he feels when Linda gives him a new toy.

"There's so much. There are 486 steps. I wasn't counting. I just know. And I know this city was founded and built by Vanthis, a dreamer of unmatched imagination, who tricked the gods into revealing some of their secrets. I know the favorite food of the buopoths who graze along the banks of the Oukranos, and the call to make that eases their fear."

As he speaks, the smile stretches crazily across his face. His eyes glaze.

"Oh, there's so much! The shadowy intersections of dream and waking. And why the ghouls can move freely between them. And the language of the nightgaunts. And where all of the tunnels beneath dread Sarkomand lead. And—"

"Can you tell me where we need to go?" asks Jake eagerly.

Ben sputters and blinks. His eyes refocus on the excited dog before him.

"Hmm. I don't know. If you can tell me what it is you're trying to find, I can probably tell you where to go. But you don't know, do you?"

"No. Sandy doesn't, either. Or Algernon."

"Then I'm sorry, but I can't help with that." Standing up, he says, "But I can do the job that I'm here for. Are you ready?"

When Jake nods, Ben lifts him up.

With that tower room far above the tops of the city walls, it's easy to pick out the window facing east. The pleasant warmth of the sun can be felt the moment Jake's head and front legs are placed into the opening. A few inches later his shoulders are the first roadblock. Scrunching them together gives him the clearance he needs—until his ribcage becomes the issue. Front paws can feel the outside edge. Gripping as best he can with his claws, he exhales and pulls forward...

He's out!

Far enough, anyway. His hips block him from going further.

Wedged in stone, the ground hundreds of feet below, Jake's not sure if this is better than being taken aloft by vulture. At least, there's no way for him to fall. The intensity of the sun is muted by hazy cirrus clouds, allowing him to see a blanket of green extending to the horizon, the river snaking through it.

Ben's voice floats out through the crack.

"Are you okay?"

With the bottom of his ribcage digging against the sharp edges of the stone, it's definitely past *uncomfortable* and into *painful* territory. But he can put up with it for a while longer, and the man's hands reassure him that the normalcy of inside isn't far away at all.

"I'm okay."

Calming himself, glad of Ben's company, he recalls what had happened with the vulture: The specific odor of the bad thing hadn't registered until he brought back the memory of his first encounter with it in the park. Locking that in his mind, he inhales and analyzes.

For the most part, a light breeze comes from the south. When it blows, there is no trace of that odor. All he can smell is river and the ships at the dock, and beyond that, trees.

But when the wind calms, much more can be identified. Minute traces. People and animals, mainly, in all directions. From the west, Zoogs. In the south, something that smells like sheep. Maybe it's the buopoths that Ben mentioned. And...

East!

It's there, then blown away as the wind picks up again. There is no doubt, but to be sure, Jake waits for another period of stillness. After getting it, he feels more confident: east for sure, but, based on the sun, a little north of straight east.

"Pull me back, Ben."

A firm tug on his hips does no good. A second, with Jake emptying his lungs, also fails. And the third. While catching his breath, he feels a hand firmly, but gently, worm its way between his ribcage and the stone of the sill. Through the opening above, the other grabs his shoulder. Together, they work the tissues to slide bone and cartilage past the sticking point.

His upper body squeezed, unable to breathe at all, Jake starts to panic. With only his rear legs able to move, they spasm wildly, clawing at the wall. But those paws find a purchase. Steady pressure from his legs, added to Ben's efforts, overcomes the friction. He moves. And with a swoosh he's safely in Ben's arms!

Grateful, the aches in his ribs and shoulders easing already, he plies Ben with exuberant licks. Laughing, the man accepts them all, then sets Jake down.

But that energy can't be dismissed that easily. Flopping over, he scratches his back against the floor, tail beating wildly. And in that position, there's a treat of belly rubs as well. Granted, much of his joy is the sheer relief of being safely inside and having done his job, but added in is the happiness of being with a new friend.

He's so nice!

Nice, or trustworthy, or friendly. Any or all of those words are good. Jake will always think of Sandy as his closest companion, and he adores Linda. But Ben provides something different, something that's been missing from his life. And that connection is such a wonderful feeling.

"I smelled it," Jake tells him, standing up. "The bad thing is in the east, like it was before."

"East? That whittles it down. Unless your nose can smell something from the other side of the Cerenarian Sea, all that lies between it and Thran is a land known as Kled."

"Kled? What's there?"

"Jungle, mainly. There are ancient temples that are reputed to be haunted. Or cursed. But according to what I learned on the trip up, they're really not. Do you want to start down? I'll tell you on the way."

"I'm ready to go."

But, as soon as the man's shoe touches the first step, he stops and looks back. Jake can see his brow furrow.

"What about Kled?" prompts Jake.

"Oh, the temples. They were. They were built. A long time ago. By… Well, the name isn't important. Anyway, they—"

Facing forward, he takes a second step. And stops again. When Jake cranes his neck around, he can see Ben's mouth hanging open.

Cautiously, another step.

"Oh no," he moans, grabbing his head with both hands. "I know what the curse is."

"What is it?" whimpers Jake.

"On the trip up, I learned…so much. Going back down, the knowledge is…erased. Ripped out. It feels— It feels more terrible than I could imagine. In my mind. Holes."

The fourth step, and a pause.

The fifth. Pause.

Jake hears a sob that tears at his heart.

After a deep breath, Ben starts and keeps going, right hand on the wall, left on his head. Jake falls in behind him. The pace is slow, but they're moving.

It's a long way down.

Seeing his new friend suffer, unable to do anything to help, had been excruciating for Jake. Ben, though still walking, still alive, appears barely so. He'd plainly sacrificed a piece of himself—or, hopes Jake, it is only a piece. Is it possible to heal from something like he described?

With his feet on the floor at the very bottom, Ben looks around at the cats and dogs. "Goodbye," he mouths before shuffling away. No one tries to stop him. When he reaches the top of the short flight of stairs, Ariadne tilts her head at two of the cats. They chase after the broken man.

"The curse?" she asks Jake. "Is he affected by the curse?"

He nods.

"Did he say anything about it?"

"He said," sighs Jake, "that he learned things on the way up. A lot. He was very, very happy to know everything. But..." He swallows the sorrow stuck in his throat. "But it all got taken back out on the way down. He said he had holes in his head. Inside."

"Cruel," remarks Ariadne.

"When is a curse not cruel?" asks Algernon. There are head shakes all around. "Was his sacrifice worthwhile? Were you able to do what you needed?"

"I was," replies Jake. "It's east mainly, and a little north. Ben said something about a place named Kled."

Algernon hangs his head.

Catching that reaction, Sandy glares at the cat. "Did he really need to help you?" she asks Jake.

"He did. Maybe I could've jumped up and wiggled through. Maybe. But I'd be stuck without him to pull me back in." Unable to contain it, a wail escapes. "I wish Ben didn't have holes in his head!"

Sandy frowns and turns to the cat.

"Algernon! Will you finally admit to knowing that we needed to go to this Kled all along?"

"I could not be certain," insists the cat. "The odds were very good, but it is critical that we not waste time following an imaginary scent."

"But we have wasted plenty of time this morning. And needlessly sacrificed a good ally."

"You are right. More than the morning, this entire day is lost. I hadn't anticipated spending this much time in the tower. Kled is not far from here, but it would be a mistake to end that journey in the dark. We will spend another night in Thran and set out in the morning."

"Good. Jake and I will stay at the inn tonight."

"We will?" asks Jake.

"We will."

Algernon's eyebrows rise.

"As you wish," he concedes. "I need to plan a battle strategy with Ariadne. Your presence is not required for that. Be prepared to leave at dawn."

Even as the cats maneuver the two dogs through the sea of humanity and back to *The Broken Goat*, Jake wonders if he wants to see Ben again so soon. Grief having taken a greater toll than the physical exertion, he'd been looking forward to sleeping the rest of the day away, trying to not think about the despondent man.

Upon arriving at the ancient inn, the cats depart. Sandy scratches on the door, then yaps twice.

When it opens, Howard sticks his head out.

"Oh, you two again?" The tone of his voice is kind, but there's confusion, as well. "Where's your friend, the cat?"

Sandy provides a single yip of explanation.

"Hmm."

Leaving the door cracked, he yells inside.

"Phylla! It's the two dogs from this morning I told you about. But without the cat. Should I invite them in?"

Footsteps approach and the door swings fully open to reveal a thin woman, taller than her mate. Long, white curls hang far past her shoulders, but her skin is smooth and youthful. She looks the pair up and down, her jaw set in a way that reminds Jake of Linda when she is not in a mood for foolery. But at the same time, those stern eyes radiate warmth.

"You will behave yourselves in our home?"

A subdued "woof" from each are enough to convince her.

"Then come in. We will trust you to mind your manners."

Except for a couple sitting quietly on the far side of the room, the place is empty. Sandy dashes straight to the window table where they had met Ben.

"The young man is in his room, upstairs," says Howard.

"He seems to be very upset," adds Phylla.

Jake, next to the stairs, sniffs at the bottom-most step. Ben's anguish lies thick on the wood, as if it had dripped off of him.

There's so much. Too much. Unwilling to deal with it, he turns away and sits down near the door. His eyes meet Sandy's. Expecting her to say something, she instead turns and makes her way up.

"You're friends of him, then?" asks Phylla.

Jake tries to smile and manages a half-wag.

"A loyal dog is all the treasure a man needs, especially a troubled one. You can go up to see him."

He forces himself to stand, walk over. Sandy is most of the way up. But that odor of despair, almost palpable, draws a whine out of him.

Can't.

Backing up, he returns to his spot by the door and lies down.

"Oh, you poor dear. You're as upset as he. Ben is very generous with his coin every time he stays. We'll return the favor and feed you later. How does that sound?"

The promise of human food elicits a full wag.

When the innkeepers go, Jake turns his attention to what is happening out of sight upstairs. He hears Sandy scratch at the door. Again. And again. A creak. Sandy's toenails on the wooden floor. Another creak, and a thump-click of the door. Regret wells up in Jake, but it's too late to overcome exhaustion. He curls up. His eyes close.

Something wakes him.

Two voices upstairs, talking?

Maybe. He doesn't care. It's not time to eat. His eyes close again.

Food!

As Jake opens his eyes, Howard is placing a shallow bowl on the floor. It smells delicious.

"Here you go, my friend. It's a little early, and you've been very good, but the wife and I think you should fill up now. So as to not be begging when you see the rest of the guests eat."

Wagging, Jake stands, stretches, and digs into a hearty beef stew, more meat than vegetable.

"Ben, can you send down that small dog to get some dinner?" Howard calls upstairs.

After a pause, the door creaks open. Soon, Sandy is next to him, enjoying her own, smaller portion. As they finish licking the dishes clean, people begin to enter. The innkeeper dutifully welcomes and engages with each one. Grateful for the meal, Jake eagerly looks for a chance to thank the man.

But Sandy blocks him.

"I know what you're thinking, Jake," she whispers. "We need to go outside."

The door opens and a man and woman enter.

Sandy is able to push Jake through before it shuts and leads him to the edge of the yard, away from the main walkway.

"You can't thank him," she says, voice low. "Or the woman."

"But they were so nice to us."

"It doesn't matter. You can't speak to them. You may frighten them."

"Why?"

"Because most of the people here aren't— They don't have imagination. For them, a dog has to be…"

She frowns.

"Happy and stupid," finishes Jake.

A nod.

"But not Ben," suggests Jake.

"Ben is different. He's…smarter."

"How is he?" asks Jake hesitantly.

"Not good. And if you want to thank Howard and Phylla, just act happy. If they can see that you're happy, that will be all the thanks they need."

When a boisterous group of men walk up, the dogs sit quietly until they enter. Howard's booming voice is easy to make out, and it's followed by a roar of laughter that shakes the inn.

Sighing, Jake looks up. The sky is blue straight above, but streaked with red off to the west, where the sun has sunk down behind the wall of the city.

"It feels like it'll be a comfortable night," he says. "Maybe I'll sleep out here."

"Do you want some company?"

"I'd like that."

Though its walls and spires will certainly gleam in the sun later in the day, this dawn in Thran, like all of them, is a dark affair. The sounds of innkeepers moving around inside wake the dogs. Lantern light spills out through the windows of *The Broken Goat*, along with the aroma of breakfast. Phylla comes out with a bowl of water and a few gobbets of meat.

"Here are some yummy bits for you," she says before going back inside.

It's small breakfast, but enough to start the day. As Jake and Sandy quench their thirst, Algernon shows up with Ariadne. One window in the upper floor is lit, but Jake can't tell if it's Ben's room or not. Tempted to ask Sandy, he instead holds his tongue, believing it better to try to forget about the poor, cursed man.

On the move earlier this day than they had been the previous, the journey through the town is much easier. Soon, they're at the south gate. To exit, all that the trio needs to do is pretend that they are accompanying someone. Ariadne pulls them to the side and they wait for the right opportunity to come along.

"That one," she says after a short time. "We know that family."

A man guides a mule pulling a cart. Two small girls walk with him, each with their own doll. Two dogs trail them all. With the children quarreling over the dolls, the father separates them, yanks the toys out of their hands, and swaps them.

"Just be friendly to the dogs and walk with them, behind the cart."

"I will be in touch," Algernon tells her, then scoots off. Jake and Sandy fall in line behind him.

The dogs with the cart are, of course, pleased to meet the newcomers, and even the cat. Up close, it's obvious that they're older, far less excitable. Greetings are exchanged. For Jake, the conversation is as disappointing as the last one he had, filled with "Hey" and "Who are you" and little else.

But, with no need for the guards to inspect or question the outward-bound stream, they make it through the gate without any canine complications.

Outside the soaring walls, the sun is indeed up. With the river running straight west-to-east in this spot, that warm ball is centered above it, framed by trees on either side. The clear water sparkles as if the surface is coated with diamonds.

As the cart turns right, toward Kiran, Algernon, Sandy, and Jake veer left. The other two dogs complain briefly, but, loyal to their family, they stay with the cart. Looking back, Jake watches them and wistfully wonders if being happy and stupid is so bad.

It's not, he decides. *But I like being happy and smart.*

With Algernon wanting to reach their destination as quickly as possible, they walk with the fastest pace that Sandy can keep, taking only breaks for water at convenient streams. The path itself is much the same as always, but the scenery transforms.

On their left, cultivated fields disappear not far past the city walls, replaced with an unbroken line of wild vegetation. The hues of the leaves begin to vary in striking ways, lightening to nearly yellow, darkening to nearly black. The bark of the trees grows smoother, sometimes oozing a liquid with an oddly sweet aroma.

And on the right, the river broadens. To the west of Thran there had often been stretches so rock-strewn and shallow that the water would burble like a stream. Here, on the eastern side, the water is deep enough to accommodate the ships that had been docked outside the south gate of the city.

Seeing one approach from the east, Algernon has them duck into the undergrowth. The men on board working efficiently and silently, twenty oars dip into the water as one, propelling it past them. Once it's beyond a bend, the three continue on.

The sun is directly overhead when Algernon stops them.

"Jake, please go ahead of us and see if you can find the scent of the thing."

Distracted by the sights, sounds, and smells along this stretch, numbed by the constant walking, Jake had forgotten why he was there. The request comes as a small shock.

Oh.

Wandering forward, he imagines the odor and sniffs. Nose high, there's no trace to be found amid the myriad other scents. But low? He puts his nose to the ground. The trail is packed hard and holds nothing of interest. On the left, the weeds are coated with a variety of smells, but not what he needs. To the right, the bank drops off, a severely steep fall to the water below: dead end.

He tries anyway.

Spreading his legs, he dips his head down as far as he can. That tickle returns.

There!

On the bank is the barest whiff. Heading back toward Sandy and Algernon, he tries again.

Maybe. But maybe not.

Not much further downriver, a small, rock-strewn beach allows easy access to the edge of the river. Rocketing up to that landing, he picks it out immediately. And it's a real, solid odor that registers now, not a buried memory of a scent.

"Here!" he barks back to his companions. Following the nasal clue upriver toward them, he clings to the steepening slope as far as he can. It must have kept to the river, but had undeniably touched the bank *there*. And *there*. Reversing course to the beach, he zeroes in: up the bank, across the path, and into the green.

Jake proudly points into the tall grasses. Their whole quest, previously only vaguely defined, is now more concrete.

"That way!"

But Sandy stares at something as she and Algernon join him. Obsessed with the odor, he had missed it: a line of flattened plants, as if something had been dragged.

Algernon studies that imprint as well, his tail motionless.

"We've arrived," he says. "These are the jungles of Kled."

Pleased at their progress while also recognizing the need for a rest, Algernon suggests that they take time to eat. Instead of rabbit, Jake and Sandy feast on small balls of fur that look like fat mice. Sandy calls them gerbils, and Jake is delighted with the taste. The meat is tinged with an exotic flavor that he has never had before.

After that break, the familiar, friendly river path is left behind as they penetrate into the jungle. While birds had kept them infrequent company during the recent miles, there's now a nonstop cacophony of singing and cawing and whistling. Occasionally he catches a flash of colorful wings, but the canopy of foliage overhead prevents a clear view of anything.

With the thing's passage easy to discern, they keep the same order with the cat in the lead. At a spot where the odor is particularly intense, Jake stops them and describes exactly what it is that he smells, but neither Algernon or Sandy seems to be able to pick up on the nature of the badness that he knows so intimately.

Surrounded by so many unique and wonderful aromas, Jake begins to wish he couldn't smell what he does. Becoming fouler the farther they go, the odor of that thing pollutes the aromas of the flowers and trees and rodents and birds. Sourly, it occurs to him that he's not supposed to be enjoying himself. They haven't walked all the miles that they have for fun. They're trying to track something down.

We're close, though.

It shouldn't be much longer. And when they do find it, his job will be done and the cats can take over and do whatever they need to do.

Then Sandy and I can have some fun here before we wake up.

A clearing!

For the first time in many minutes, they're not fenced in by stalks of brown and green. Above, the sun winks from behind a mask of cotton clouds and ahead lies an area covered with flat stones. Some hardy seedlings grow atop them where wind-borne debris has accumulated to create shallow pockets of soil, but none breach the joints of those perfectly fitted tiles to root into the earth below. In the center of the nearly pristine courtyard: a building made of large blocks of yellow-orange stone. White and gold accents gleam when the sun peeks out. Statues are positioned along the eastern and western walls of the structure, each with the body of a person and the head of an animal. Jake can easily identify a cat, a dog, and several birds. The others, some very fearsome looking, are alien to him.

The only detail that jars the eye is the ugly gash in the ground surrounding the temple—though it's not the gap itself that is the issue. With even lines and sharp edges, the quality perfectly matches the rest of the complex. The less-than-attractive portion is the contents of that ditch, the still water covered almost completely in a slimy layer of algae.

On the western side, a bridge spans that foul water. A single arch made of the same stone, there's a gentle curve up, then down. And it's the only way across, they learn as Algernon leads them past it and they are able to clearly see that the north side of the building is as featureless as the south.

Not smelling a need to go any farther, Jake stops.

"The trail goes over the bridge," he says, pointing his nose at it.

But when the cat moves toward it, the dogs do not.

"Everything will be fine," Algernon assures them, and starts forward again.

An eyebrow raise from Jake is answered by a nod from Sandy.

"Is this some sort of temple?" Sandy asks the cat.

"Yes. It's the—It's very old."

From above, the contents of the moat look more disgusting. In those rare places where actual water can be seen, it's clear, but reveals nothing of its dark depths. And although the outer edge of that artificial ravine drops straight down, the inner edge is sloped, the surface rough, allowing easy access down to the water's edge. Or, rather, the slime's edge.

At the crest of the rise, Jake gets a look at the inside through the entrance ahead—as far as he can, anyway. A wall set a short way in requires a turn to either right or left. And though there seems to be only the one doorway and no windows, the interior can be plainly seen, lit from within somehow.

Algernon stops them at that opening.

"Now is when we need to take care," he says, splitting them up. Jake is directed to the left side, behind a bird-headed statue, its beak curved like raptors he's seen in the park. Sandy is put behind a cat-headed one on the right.

"I'm going to call the guardian. Both of you: Be brave. And silent."

At the very edge of the transition between outside and in, the cat spins around. Gazing at the bridge and moat, he taps one rear paw on the inside floor.

From beneath that revolting water, it explodes! Armored and muck-encrusted, a mouth large enough to swallow Jake whole opens wide, revealing teeth white and terrible. Having reared high, it crashes down toward Algernon. The cat tenses, but does not move. He speaks a word. To Jake, it sounds like a purr.

"Err."

With gravity in control of the trajectory, it does not—cannot—stop. But the head does manage to twist far enough to the side. Instead of crushing the cat, those mammoth jaws slam down inches away. The reverberation travels up Jake's spine. He remembers seeing such beasts on the television, but doesn't know how to name them.

"We are all friends," says the cat.

Thick, stubby legs back the monstrosity up slightly. Its eyes focus on Jake, then Sandy, before returning to Algernon.

"Friends," croaks the thing.

"Chaos is at hand, however. Allowances must be made. Oaths must be suspended. Trust is key."

"Trust," it repeats, then, turning, eases back into the water. It's a long time before the tail, lined with rows of spiky scales, completely submerges.

"You two can come out now," says Algernon. "The guardian will not threaten us again."

"Guardian?" asks Jake. "So, it's on our side? It's good?"

"Crocodiles are neither good nor evil. That one has a job to do: protect this temple. And it doesn't care how good or how bad you are when it eats you."

"Was that a password you spoke?" asks Sandy.

"It was. We are free to enter."

"But we don't need to," she says.

Algernon's eyes narrow. "We need to prove that the thing is inside."

"It's needlessly risky," she argues. "There is only the trail across the bridge. Hidden or invisible, it must be here." Her eyes scanning all around, she adds, "Just standing here probably isn't safe."

"I need proof," states the cat.

"May the rats eat you! And your proof!"

"Don't fight!" barks Jake. "I'll go in."

Sandy glares at him.

"But once I smell it inside, we can go?" he asks Algernon.

"That's right."

"Fine!" she huffs. "Go. We'll watch your back."

Carefully, Jake steps through the entrance. When the first paw touches down, he glances back at the moat.

Whew.

Inside, he can see that the roof has long gashes to allow sunlight in. And one detail becomes evident in a very short time: There is no scent of the thing.

What?

Stepping back out, he sniffs.

Yes.

Then back in, another attempt.

No.

"It's not in there," he says. "It never went in. But out here…"
It's easy to pick out that odor at the threshold. And ahead. And left. And right. Trying to nail down the location of the most intense source, Jake wanders away from the building. His head darts in every direction.

"What's wrong?" asks Algernon.

"I'm confused. Now I smell it all around us."

"All around?" asks Sandy.

As Jake tries to find better words to explain the unexplainable, they appear! Surrounding them is a ring of animals, shoulder to shoulder. Though small and furry, the collection of teeth and claws on display is frightening. As one, they launch themselves at the trio with a cacophony of screeching.

"Squirrels?" yips Jake, backing away. With the body not as long as the tree rodent, and the tail far less impressive, the only really daunting aspect is the mouth. Those pointy fangs seem to be able to do far more damage than the ones used to gnaw on nuts.

"Weasels!" shouts Sandy, struggling to both fend off her own attackers and get next to Jake.

Preoccupied with holding off too many, he leaves himself open. One looks to be close to sinking its teeth into his haunch, but Sandy is suddenly there, snagging it by the neck, then whipping her head to fling it away. Looking to weigh at least as much as she does, it flies amazingly far.

The two dogs now covering each other, they retreat back to the wall. Growling, barking, they're in a position to safely hold off the gang, but it's a stalemate. Having far too many to fight through, the pair are stuck. Minutes of slashing and gnashing ensue with neither side inflicting any damage upon the other. Jake gets the impression that they're afraid of he and Sandy, but how long can they keep this up? And there's no sign of Algernon.

"Enough," growls Sandy. She repeats what Algernon had said earlier: "Err!"

Though it doesn't rush out of the water as rapidly as before, the crocodile covers the distance quickly for being so remarkably large. Swinging its head, it bats at the weasels, knocking them away from the dogs. They retreat together, some running around, some scrambling over, the scaly body. A final thrash of the mighty tail scatters a few, but they regroup and all make it into the temple.

"Where's Algernon?" asks Jake.

"He ran inside," says Sandy. "Find the cat and bring it here," she directs the beast.

Jake is fascinated to see that it obeys her command, turning and waddling into the structure.

"Should we go in?" he asks.

"This is a task the guardian can handle alone. We'll only get in the way."

"Where did the weasels come from?"

"They were never here, Jake."

"Sure, they were. I could feel them."

"Something was here," explains Sandy. "The thing was. You found it. But disguised as a mass of weasels. In reality, it was a different shape. Probably completely different."

Bird-not-bird!

"But why?" he asks.

112

"Chaos is often a useful tool," comes Algernon's voice from the entrance.

In Jake's young life this has to be the most bizarre sight he's yet seen, even including having weasels materialize from thin air. The cat is perched on the head of the lizard as it pulls its bulk through the doorway. Jake gives it plenty of room.

Leaping off, Algernon commands it, "Begone to your watery rest."

Without pausing, the reptile continues on, sliding into and beneath the surface of the moat.

"And you two," the cat tells the dogs, "follow me."

Leading them across the bridge, Algernon struts in a way that Jake hadn't noticed before. Back on the flat courtyard, he waves a paw to have them wait, then walks to the jungle at the western edge before returning.

"I am very pleased at this development," he says. "As you may have guessed, the weasels were an illusion. A distraction. Their flight into the temple at the end was meant to mislead. As they appeared to run inside, the thing fled in the opposite direction. Jake, find the scent. Where is it strongest?"

Nose to the ground, Jake begins to make a circle around Sandy. Algernon backs up a bit. Aside from the bridge, there are two branches to the odor trail: south and west. By far the telltale scent is stronger in the west.

"That way," says Jake, pointing straight at the cat.

"Precisely," says Algernon. "Having had our encounter with the entity, as illusory as it was, I am now attuned to it. I can detect it now, and so lead."

"That means you do not need us any longer," observes Sandy.

113

That seems to take Algernon by surprise. Nose flaring, his mouth opens before silently closing again.

From Jake's perspective, he really isn't sure if that's good news or bad. There's relief because the level of danger had grown to be uncomfortably, scarily real. He could now have a chance to relax and enjoy himself. But there's also disappointment. For a while, his nose had been special. He had been more important than ever before in his life.

"Need?" says the cat after a protracted pause. "No. I don't. But I would prefer we stay together for a time. With a vicious entity on the loose, there is safety in numbers. And this world is not free of more mundane threats, as well."

"That makes sense," agrees Jake.

Sandy looks at both before nodding.

"Do you think it ran that way merely to escape?" she asks. "Or purposely? Is there anything to the west?"

"There is a destination that makes sense," replies the cat.

Jake looks past Algernon, into the claustrophobic greenery.

"Back into the jungle," he sighs.

"Only for a short while. Not far past the edge of the courtyard, there is a wide path running to the west that our prey will likely take. That route passes to the north of Thran. If you wish to part ways, you will easily be able to make your way there once those towers come into view."

"Where will you go?" asks Jake.

"If the trail leads where I suspect, to the Temple of the Night. Along with this one, the Temple of the Dawn, the pair bracketed this ancient land."

"Is that one just as *dead*?" asks Sandy.

Her emphasis perplexes Jake. The crocodile wasn't dead.

Algernon closes his eyes before speaking.

"In this age, most all is dead. Long ago, things were far different. The people of that time dared to dream. They tamed the jungle. They grew rich on the trade of the aromatic resins of its trees. Their world was smaller, the edges of their society well-defined. As were the norms of their culture. All were happy. Harmonious." That last word is spat out. "And what is harmony? Peaceful coexistence, all ideas and ideals treated equally? Hardly! None ever dare introduce a new perspective to challenge the order of the day. Any such efforts are ever squelched. Muted. Drowned!"

Eyes flashing open, he sweeps his head left and right. "Now, look! Despite their *harmonious* efforts, chaos rules. The jungle has taken over."

"There will always be conflict when incompatibilities meet," suggests Sandy.

"And there will always be a best proposition that lies above all others. Best, by definition, requires that those others submit."

"Or die?"

Standing, the cat only says, "We should travel as far as we can before the sun goes down."

For Jake, the scent is easy to follow through the vegetation. And, as Algernon had said, they do find a path before long, one made by creatures called elephants. Sandy tries to describe them, but even though she insists that they eat leaves and grass, and are harmless to dogs, the picture burned into Jake's mind is nothing short of horrific.

115

Staying far in the lead, the pace set by the cat is fierce. Jake is forced to alternate between a trot and a run to keep up. Sandy's legs are a blur, never resting for a moment. But she neither complains nor seems to tire.

Having been trampled flat by the elephants, the going is certainly easier than trying to push through untamed jungle, but obstacles do remain. Branches that the mighty beasts can step over or squash either need to be slunk under or climbed atop. The streams they come upon have no bridges. Twice, a short swim is necessary. And these waters aren't anywhere near as wholesome as what they'd had in the vicinity of Kiran and Thran. Here, the taste carries with it a faint corruption. A single dip of his tongue to wet his mouth is all that Jake dares.

But, worst of all, the footprints in softer ground that Sandy can fit wholly within only reinforce to Jake the monstrousness of the things that made them.

With the sun down, Algernon finally pauses beside an outcropping of rock.

"We will not be able to make our destination this day," he says. "Being exposed in this place at night is not wise. The two of you will be safe in there."

Peering into the shadows, Jake sees what seems to be a good sleeping spot: cozy, set into the stone to provide a roof, and with no cracks to hide any nasty, bity things.

"And what will you do?" asks Sandy.

"I will scout ahead. The scent is fresh."

The cat scampers off, into the dusk.

"I'm so tired," yawns Jake. "How does he keep going?"

"He must be excited to be on the trail of the thing."

"Too excited for me. Can we have some gerbils again, then get some sleep?"

"We can," replies Sandy. "But would you like to try this time?"

"Can I? How do you do that?"

"This place is different from the waking world," Sandy begins, then pauses for a moment. "Things can be made to happen. Mind you, not everything. Impossible is still impossible, no matter how much you may want it. And you always have to consider the others that are here. You must refrain from— Share. Think in terms of sharing. Food and water are easy, though, and it's time you tried it. Imagine a gerbil somewhere close by."

Jake does. But, recalling their noontime meal, he zeroes in on the meat itself, not the living, furry thing that it had once been. The result reaches their noses at the same time.

"Oof," wheezes Jake. Of all the nauseating odors he's experienced, this is one of the worst. Not far away, easily located, the decomposing gerbil has been stripped of most of its fur. The muscle and innards are teaming with maggots and beetles. It's hard to say which is more stomach-churning: the sight or the smell.

"We need to bury it," says Sandy, curling her nose.

Inspired to be rid of the thing, Jake hurriedly digs a hole a short distance from the pile of rotten meat. With a stick that Sandy finds, they take turns poking at it from different angles. At length, the mess is at the bottom of the hole. After covering it, the stench lingers, but is tolerable.

"Do you know what went wrong, Jake?"

The question is not unforeseen. He did do something wrong. But what?

117

Think.

The pressure to figure it out builds. He's not stupid. He's not. *Think!*

In the near darkness he meets Sandy's gaze. Her eyes are kind, but expectant, awaiting an answer.

Gerbils. Rabbits. They ran. Chase. We chased them! There's always a chase.

Confident, but nervous, he asks, "It needed to be alive?"

"That's right!"

Jake smiles.

"It makes little sense for a dead animal of any kind to be found, ready to eat," explains Sandy. "That is an example of the impossible I mentioned. Are you ready to try again?"

Nodding, he stares at a bush and imagines how the live gerbil he'd seen had looked and acted.

And there one is!

It's out in the open, but sees the predator and takes off—not quickly enough, though. With a pounce and snap, he has it.

"Good, Jake. Very well done."

In two bites, it's down.

"Do you want one?" he pants eagerly. "I can do it again. I could use another one."

"I'm sure you can. But before you do that, let's try something different. There are plenty of rats in this jungle."

"Rat? Ugh. I didn't think you liked rat."

"City rat? No, I don't. But wild rat? That's better than gerbil."

Intrigued by the notion, Jake waits while Sandy shuts her eyes. When she opens them, they narrow, focusing on something behind him. Hearing the crack of a twig being stepped upon, he turns his neck.

What?!

Larger than Sandy, it lunges toward Jake. Startled, he twists out of the way as she shoots forward. Her aim is perfect. Grabbing the rat by the throat, locked on, she whips her body back and forth, nearly bringing it down. Recovered from the shock, Jake leaps on top and adds his strength. His canines pierce flesh and the blood seeps into his mouth.

Awful!

He's forced to let go. Hacking and spitting, he tries to rid himself of the acridity that is so very similar to the deer that Algernon had summoned for the vulture.

When the rat stops wriggling, Sandy releases her grip.

"I'm sorry, Jake. I forgot. It's another taste that needs to be acquired."

"I can't believe you li—" He catches some movement, the fat belly of the rat pulsing slightly. "It's still alive."

"It's not," she assures him, then, teeth bared, punctures the thin skin of the abdomen and yanks ferociously. Tiny, unborn young spill out, perfectly sized mouthfuls for the small dog.

And, to Jake's astonishment, she feasts. One by one, Sandy picks them out of the womb, crunches the fragile bones, and swallows. Most go quietly, though one manages a frail squeak right before its end.

For Jake, the image is so surreal that he has to wonder if he's dreaming. Then he realizes that yes, he is. He is dreaming, and there is no way that Sandy would do such a thing in real life. But, with blood-matted fur around her mouth painting a black mask upon her in the low light, she looks mysterious and intimidating. And far less fragile than he knew her to be. Or, *thought* he knew her to be.

And now her jaws are working on the ribs, then below them. Plucking out the liver, she swallows that as well.

And she's done, finally, stuffing far more into her tiny body than it seemed to be possible.

She did really run a lot today, though.

"Are you sure you don't want any?" she asks, licking her chops. "The only way to learn to appreciate a strange or new flavor is to force yourself to eat it even when you do not."

His appetite, any desire to gobble up another gerbil… It's all gone.

"None for me," he mumbles, heading toward the nook.

"Get some sleep. We should take turns, only one of us asleep at a time. Two shifts apiece should do it."

"To watch for elephants?" gulps Jake.

"Forget about the elephants, Jake. Just stay out of their way. You don't want one to accidentally step on you. Snakes are far worse. They'll slither in here and squeeze the life out of you, then swallow you whole."

Try as he might, he can't picture that. For something Sandy-sized or cat-sized however…

"What about Algernon?"

"Don't worry about him. He knows these lands. I have a feeling he won't have a problem with serpents tonight."

Somehow, he is able to get a bit of sleep before being woken up for his first turn. Perhaps Sandy's unexpected savagery, while

120

disturbing to witness, had also allowed him to feel safe enough to relax.

At first paying attention to the nonstop barrage of night noises, he grows accustomed to the chirps and cries of the canopy above, and the shifting rustle of leaves lower down. At length, the endless, harmless repetition makes him weary.

His eyes lower, half-way.

Then open.

A shadow he'd been staring at detaches itself from the rest of the darkness, resolves into something cat-like, but larger.

As he freezes still, the creature dashes over to the remains of the dead rat, sniffs it, then hauls it away. Whatever it was had stayed far enough away, but that potential threat gives him the motivation to pay closer attention. Everything seems to be bigger here: birds, rats, cats. That crocodile. And snakes, according to Sandy. And the mysterious elephants…

When he feels the moon has traveled far enough across the sky, he wakes Sandy.

His second shift is even more exciting than the first. Knowing that this place is far more harmful than he had originally imagined, and with the moon down, his eyes struggle to make sense of the patterns of different shades of blackness.

But it's not a sight in the pre-dawn light that causes his paws to itch with alarm. Rather, it's a sound. Branches that he knows to be far off the ground scratch against an enormous body. Between those swishes there's a soft rustle of steps of something approaching boldly. No. Somethings.

More than one!

He picks out movement, a writhing in in the darkness, feet off the ground.

Snake!

And curved slashes of white hover in the air on either side of the snake.

What?

A mountain of grey, more massive than any car he's ever ridden in, lumbers toward him. The snake—a trunk, Sandy had named it—is attached where the nose would be, between two tusks. The face is framed by ears the size of bed pillows.

THAT's what an elephant is?

On the television they had looked smaller. Sandy sure made them sound different.

One by one, of all sizes, they tromp by. A younger, smaller one looks through the weeds and seems to take notice of the dog looking back out. It stops and they lock eyes for a brief second, but a larger one forces it into motion again.

By the time the train ends, the sky is growing lighter with the dawn. Jake creeps out of his hole and watches them blend into the jungle, heading east.

With Sandy's surprising taste preference of the night before, and now armed with the knowledge of how to get food, Jake has his own breakfast of gerbils before she wakes. Having no interest in discovering any more secrets about his friend, he discretely explores or looks away while she dines.

Algernon appears shortly after she finishes.

"We went farther yesterday than I had planned," he says. "The tips of the spires of Thran are glinting in the sunlight east of south." When Jake looks in what he thinks is the right direction, the cat adds, "Within these trees, you'll need to climb one to be high enough to glimpse them."

"Where is the temple you mentioned yesterday?" asks Sandy.

"Perhaps four hours away at a walking pace. As some caution should be exercised, there is no need to hurry."

For Jake, the jungle has turned out to be nerve-wracking, but the thrill of seeing elephants has him wishing for more, similar excitement.

"Are we going with you?" he asks.

"Do what you will," says Algernon. "You may backtrack east for a time, then go south to Thran, although the trees are densely packed and have grown tall, making navigation based upon sight of the towers difficult. Going farther west, a course south will take you to Kiran, though there are marshes and extra care must be taken with a variety of hazards."

Neither of those options sound very good to Jake, especially the second one. Sandy studies the cat, an odd expression on her face.

"However," adds Algernon, "if you are willing, I would value your company, your fangs, and your claws."

Sandy finally nods.

"Okay," says Jake.

That desire for more excitement wears off rapidly.

The easy travel afforded by the elephant trail does not last very long and they have to force their way through the undergrowth again. Being abnormally thick and tangled in this area, every couple of inches forward seems to bring a new danger. Once, a misstep lands Jake's front left paw on a thorn, jabbing him between the toes. Another time, a lengthy detour is required to bypass a horde of ants that is busy breaking down the remains of something cat-sized. Too little of the brown fur is visible beneath the blanket of insects to try to guess at what it had been.

And snakes are perched everywhere! Brightly colored, most are far enough above for him to feel safely out of their striking distance, but one…Hanging from a lower bough that is bent from its crushing weight, the mouth is easily large enough to swallow Sandy. When he points it out, her only, hushed comment is, "That one isn't fully grown."

But by far, the worst moment comes when they come to a stream too wide to leap. Algernon finds a way across: a fallen tree touching the near bank and getting within an easy jump of the far one. He crosses first, followed by Sandy, neither having an issue. But Jake has a difficult time keeping his feet on the narrow, wet trunk. Most of the way across, an adjacent log with a flat top tempts him with easier footing.

The touch of one paw is enough to make it move, but not because it's sinking. The thing is twisting around to bite him! Reptilian jaws spring open just as Sandy barks. Jake reacts in time, getting a clawhold on the slippery wood and vaulting toward the shore. He splashes in, short of land, but clambers out of the water in plenty of time, the crocodile blocked by the tree.

With the novelty of the jungle now completely drowned out by terror over the things that dwelt within it, Jake wants nothing more than to wake up within the safety of his own home. Regretting the decision to accompany Algernon, he plods on behind the others.

It's well before noon when they arrive. In all not a long trip, Jake's nonstop trepidation had multiplied each minute into several.

As with the Temple of the Dawn, this one also has a court-yard—of sorts. A sea of dead, black sand begins where the living green ends. Obscenely clean, nothing grows within. The building at the center looks to be the same shape as the other, and with an array of statues around the outside, but that's where the similarities end. The single entrance is set in the east wall this time and the stones are a dull, dark brown, sparsely accented with gold. There is no moat, instead those black grains touching the structure itself.

Algernon hardly pauses before quitting the confines of the jungle.

Bounding after the cat, Sandy passes and blocks him.

"You spoke of exercising caution!" she hisses.

"We only need watch that one door. The scent leads into it."

"And what of a guardian? Is there one here?"

"The ancient knowledge is clear on that. Not a single guardian is here. Do you see one?"

"We didn't see the other until it was atop us."

"You need not fear a crocodile. If we can verify—"

"We?" she barks. "And now you ask us to go within?"

Clenching his jaw, Algernon glares at her before answering.

"For a short way," he says, enunciating those syllables. "I will continue to lead and so be the most vulnerable to any attack. The moment we know that the entity is within, we shall exit. I will stay here and monitor its movements, and would only ask that

125

you get word to reinforcements to meet me. At that point, your responsibilities are complete. You have my word."

When Sandy nods and steps aside, the cat continues on. But, unmoving, she closes her eyes.

Jake walks up to her quietly, afraid to interrupt her thinking or concentrating. The idea of going inside has him more than a little reticent. There are no windows to be seen. And with the interior masked in complete shadow a few feet past the doorway, there cannot be a hole in the roof as with the other one.

Can't see anything…

But more than simple darkness, the place conveys an atmosphere of not-at-all-welcome that causes his fur to stand. As Algernon gets farther from them, Jake's canine nature kicks in. He doesn't like to disappoint anyone, even a cat.

We're here. We may as well finish.

Sandy's eyes open.

"Are we going in?" Jake asks her.

"Is the odor still with us, headed inside?"

"It is. And very strong. Algernon is tracking it perfectly."

The cat stops and looks back when his name is spoken.

"Lead on," she says to the cat. "We're coming." To Jake she whispers, "If something goes wrong, remember to hold your breath."

"What?" he asks with a head tilt.

"Hold your breath," she repeats. "Let's go."

With the dogs in motion, the cat covers the final stretch of sand, pausing at the opening. Sandy and Jake are a fair distance away when Algernon's paw touches the floor inside.

A shooshing from behind is the first indication that something is happening. Looking back, Jake sees the sand stir. Many pairs of scarlet pincers poke up in the area they had passed through. Then the Sandy-sized bodies emerge, each sporting legs and more legs. The tails are terrifying, curving forward to hang over the creatures, a lethal-looking stinger at the tip.

"Scorpions!" yelps Sandy, already running. "Get inside!"

And Jake barrels after her. But, to his credit, having learned from the attack of the fake weasels at the previous temple, the first thought that races through his mind is a natural consequence.

Are they real?

Far larger than any bug he's ever seen, the skittering, red things don't seem so. But those stingers look far too formidable to find out. And Sandy seems to be genuinely frightened.

Inside, the trio are encased in darkness almost instantly. The stench of the mysterious thing they've been following is markedly heavy in the enclosed space, but despite that nasal proof for Jake, the menace posed by it is abstract, unknown. A far more immediate danger is on their tail.

A twisting look back gives him a view of the scorpions, their dreadful shapes outlined against the entrance light, but also throws him off balance. Sliding on the smooth stone, he falls and shoots to the left. There's a collision with something soft, along with the yowl of a cat. Entangled with Algernon, his sinuses overloaded with the bad scent, he is near panic as he rights himself.

"Jake!"

Orienting himself toward Sandy's voice, he manages to get a purchase on the slick floor. And does, barely, but plows into Algernon again, who's trying to go in the opposite direction.

"Here!" yells Sandy.

The staccato ticks of the scorpions closing in grant him the determination to push the cat.

The relief of reaching Sandy is short-lived. He doesn't even have time to ask, "What now?" when the floor beneath them tilts.

A lot.

Too far.

They slide.

Down, down, down.

Staying in contact with stone, occasionally bumping into the other two, their tumbling trip is never really a fall…until, sadly, it is.

The stone ends. Blind in the utter darkness, unable to feel anything except for wind rushing past, Jake's not sure if this is better or worse than the end of his trip with the vulture. Then Sandy's reminder floats back.

Hold my breath!

Instead of a splat, there's a splash!

As Jake bobs back to the surface, gasping and frantic, he strains to see anything at all in the darkness. Spinning around, he does find something. A stripe of blurry green doesn't seem to be too far away. He swims toward it.

With the water having drained from his ears, sounds register. Mainly he hears, from behind him, other things splashing in.

Plunk. Plunk-plunk.

Scorpions!

Hoping they can't swim—and praying that one doesn't land on him—he doubles his effort. The greenness gets closer. He hears other sounds: the quiet whoosh of waves lapping a shore, the dry-off shake of a dog that can only be Sandy.

His paws touch bottom.

Out of the water, he shakes off as well. Barring two animal-shaped patches of blackness, the land glows dimly everywhere he looks.

"Are we all uninjured?" asks the Sandy-shape on his right.

"I'm okay," acknowledges Jake.

"I am also fine," seethes the Algernon-shape on the other side, further away. "Why are we down here? There was an exit to the left. If you had but accompanied—"

"If you had but spoken up," Sandy rebukes him, "we may have. This is a solution to a problem that we weren't supposed to have had. Your information regarding the temple was incomplete."

"Not incomplete. Rather, subject to interpretation. As you saw for yourself, there was not one guardian, but a multitude."

His backpedaling elicits a growl from Sandy, but the bickering stops. In that calm, Jake realizes that he hasn't heard the splash of a falling scorpion for a while.

"Can those things swim?" he asks.

"They'll sink," spits Sandy. "And that water is deep."

"Okay. Good. Where are we?"

"This is the underworld. It extends underneath the entire upper world of dream."

"Can we get out?"

Sandy says nothing.

"We can," replies the cat. "But should we? It is also here."

"It?" she asks.

"The entity."

"It fell with us?"

"With, or before."

"Which direction?" Sandy asks Jake. "Where is the scent?"

It's easy to find.

"That way. Where Algernon is."

"Somehow," she mutters, "that is not the least bit surprising."

Through the darkness, they slog on.

The green glow, some kind of fragile coating, covers a greater portion of the rocks and dirt. Most of their steps dislodge at least a small amount, leaving behind a broken trail of black dots and coating their paws.

Being underground, Jake expects some echoes from the roof of the cave. But an experimental "woof" fades away with no feedback, while also drawing admonishments from both Algernon and Sandy. How far down had they slid, then fallen? The roof must be very high, indeed.

The flat landscape allows for relatively easy travel, though they do gain some elevation as they go. Atop a mild rise, a look back reveals the line of their prints leading to a large, black smear: the water. It's like the pond in the park, but much vaster. With that source far behind, Jake wonders if they'll come across a stream.

Later, he's still wondering.

How much later?

It's impossible to say. All sense of the passage of time had ceased.

He doesn't know where he is, or where he's going.

130

Thirsty, hungry, tired, the young dog is fed up and wants nothing more than for the nightmare to end. Their pursuit of the creature—or entity, as Algernon keeps referring to it—seems to be pointless. The thing is always a step ahead of them: not far, but also never able to be identified. Or touched. Had it ever been real, even when he'd been awake, in the park? Has it only been a vague concept all along? A ghostly threat of evil, only imagined?

But, making him most miserable is the feeling of being abandoned. Algernon is so far in front that he's only discernable—and barely—by gazing at the far end of the line of dots he lays down. And Sandy has been morose ever since they swam ashore, either ignoring or shushing him each time he tries to speak with her. There's been no conversation, only endless, silent walking.

Can it get any worse?

Apparently, it can.

Ahead, Algernon is waiting next to a line where the ground doesn't glow. Jake's first thought is of a pond or lake. But, picking up a parallel line of faint luminescence from the other side of that gap, it seems more likely to be a stream or river.

Closer, he can tell that's not the case either. That cavernous gash holds no water. Flecks of the omnipresent glow can be seen in the curving sides, but much more obviously in the rubble at the bottom. The ravine runs to the limit of his vision to the left, though it seems to come to an end not too far away on the right.

"You idiot!" bawls Sandy. "Where have you led us? We must be near the Vale!"

"I merely go where the scent leads," replies Algernon, backing away from the dogs. Then all defensiveness vanishes. "And I am not the one who deposited us into this black pit of horrors."

"Those scorpions were not to be trifled with!" she counters. "Flight was the only recourse!"

"Hush!" chides Algernon. "Before you—"

A rumbling tremor catches his attention.

"Which direction?" asks Sandy, voice shaking. "Where?"

Listening doesn't help at all, with the sound pitched so low. And his eyes are practically useless as a means of seeing details, but Jake realizes that, like their footprints and the ravine, it works well enough when trying to detect a *lack* of something. He looks all around for a splotch of black in the ever-present green glow.

There.

Algernon had been in the way, but at some unknown distance beyond the cat is a shape. Only able to distinguish the portion of the thing in contact with the ground, he's unable to guess at its size. But, based on that width, it's titanic.

Jake doesn't get a chance to speak even a word, though. Algernon is suddenly racing towards, between, past them! Surprised by the move, Jake gasps. And smells—it! The air is now suffocatingly thick with the odor of the thing.

"Sandy," he coughs, "it ran past us! It must be Algernon!"

"Go! Stay on his tail!"

Jake takes off at full speed. And, running beside him, Sandy keeps pace!

Relying on scent and pawprints, they tear after the fleeing cat, the earth thrumming with the motions of the unknown behemoth behind. Straight along the lip of the ravine they go until they come to a mound of soil heaped around a gargantuan hole. The trail of the cat skirts that feature, running widdershins, then heads out across flat, open terrain.

"Wait!" shouts Sandy. "Here!"

Skidding to a stop behind the pile of debris, she cozies into a crevice and scrunches down. Jake reverses course and wedges himself in next to her. Both deeply winded, they try to pant quietly.

As the rumbling draws closer, the wait becomes torturous. Pebbles drizzle down the pile onto them. Afraid of moving a single muscle, Jake wonders if he's going to be eaten or simply flattened.

Finally, it reaches them…and goes past. To Jake, it looks more than anything like a snake the length of a train. And a spot of good news for a change: It veers a little to the right, away from where they want to go. He can feel Sandy relax, and he does so as well—although it's quite a long while until the entire thing slithers by.

"I was hoping it wasn't interested in us," whispers Sandy. "It was just a coincidence showing up then."

"That wasn't a big snake, was it?" asks Jake, standing up and shaking off the dust.

"It's called a Dhole," says Sandy, also cleaning herself. "Not much is known about them except that they inhabit a certain valley. And we're in it. We'll have to be careful until we get out."

"There is a way out?"

"Yes."

"Where?"

"I don't know."

Jake whimpers.

"But the thing we chase likely does," Sandy assures him. "We need only continue after it."

"Has it… Has it been Algernon the whole time?"

"No," she says. "Only since the weasel attack. And…" She hangs her head and pauses before looking up again. "I must…apologize."

"For what?"

"I suspected that wasn't the real Algernon but was not sure. And I was afraid to warn you. I needed to see where he would go and how he would react."

"It sure looked like Algernon. But didn't act like him, now that I think about it. He kept staying far ahead of us. The one we first met wasn't as friendly as a dog, but was okay for a cat." Hesitantly, he asks, "Is the real one dead?"

"Probably not," she says. Then her tone becomes more decisive. "No, the real Algernon is definitely not dead. I believe he is a prisoner. We need to rescue him. Can you help me? Are you ready?"

For Jake, not helping is not an option.

"Ready!" he says, sniffing. "This way!"

His enthusiasm wears off rapidly. The route is largely flat, but pockmarked with holes and crisscrossed with gouges like with their first encounter. The Algernon-thing had avoided the deeper channels, staying up on the rims, but had crossed shallower ones, down one slope and up the other.

To break up the tedium, they vary their pace, switching between walking, trotting and running. Jake sometimes pushes himself to his top speed for short stretches—with Sandy keeping up.

Knowing that's impossible in the awake world, he chalks it up to the queerness of this dream place.

Rumblings of the Dholes force them to slow, or even stop, at times. And once, one of the things bursts up through the surface only a house-length in front of them before heading off to the right. When the leading end is far enough away, they move around the hole and pick up the scent on the other side.

And they walk. And trot. And run.

Something different!

Jake had grown more and more despondent during their trudge of the past hours. The normal pangs of hunger and thirst had taken hold, but the monotonously flat plain, punctuated only with Dhole tracks, had been the worst. The dull green glow, combined with the complete ignorance of their destination, had worn him down.

Is it a good thing, however, for the element of difference to be a layer of discarded bones? The uneven carpet grows denser as they go, forcing them to slow in order to keep from stumbling over the grisly obstacles. Many are so old that hardly a wisp of odor clings to them, but when it is there, it's easy to identify: human. At least, most are.

Of the others, Jake doesn't find any trace of Zoog, the only scent in this dream world that he can associate with a known creature. All he can tell is that the bones had been part of something shaped like a person, but much bulkier. At least, he gets that impression.

Maneuvering through the field, another feature soon becomes evident: a mass of stone lies ahead, marked where the bodies of the Dholes have rubbed, scraping away the green. The scent of the Algernon-thing leads right up to the rock.

No. *Into* it.

The vertical wall has a crack barely wide enough for Jake, though not anywhere near as tight as the window at the top of the tower in Thran. Within, a natural ramp leads upward, set at about the same angle as the stairs in his home. It changes directions often, twisting and turning randomly. But past the first bend, the surrounding stone bare of any glow, he is forced to rely on his whiskers as never before.

Up.

They make slow progress through that entombing blackness. When they began, Jake had been able to spot tiny flecks of green glow on the rock, likely having fallen from the paws of the false Algernon. But here, farther up, those barely-seen tidbits are few and far between. And, though the way had been entirely safe to that point, not having proof of solid ground beneath his paws shakes his confidence. Every so often he has to quash the fear of a completely undetectable hole.

Up.

He had begun this journey by descending from the mist into the cavern, where he had met the priest, Kaman-Thah. From there, the long staircase had taken them lower. Then they'd fallen through the floor of the second temple, splashing down into the water. Surely, they couldn't sink any farther. The way out of this strange and hostile land lies in the opposite direction.

Up.

The promise of waking provides the energy to continue the unending climb, despite protesting muscles and empty stomach and dirt-dry mouth.

Up.

Each step takes him farther from that terrible valley and the gigantic Dholes. And closer to home.

Up.

Up is good.

"NO!" barks Jake. His parched throat screams back at him.

They had arrived on a plateau, though still underground, and the openness had been immensely welcome. The light, too. It's brighter on this level than it had been on the valley floor. Or, maybe it only seems that way after having been effectively blind on the climb upward.

Able to find their way to the edge of the plateau, they had surveyed the lands below. There had been little to see, the only details visible being the trails of the Dholes, dark scars upon the dull green landscape. But the short break had been satisfying.

Had been.

Returning to pick up the scent again, they had discovered that it led...down. A crack in the rocks, and within, a path downward, similar to the one they had ascended. Making matters worse, Jake had spotted, not far off, a way up that is far broader than the narrow cracks. It is so inviting. *Up* means *out*, after all. A way out of the nightmare. *Down* is easily the worst alternative. It's unthinkable.

"I'm done with this, Sandy! I want to wake up! I don't care where the thing is, or what it is. Let it do whatever it wants. This is just a dream!"

Sandy frowns and shakes her head.

"Dreaming and waking are connected, Jake. Events here aren't just a dream. Effects can spread. When the pot of chaos is stirred, who can say what will be served for dinner?"

"I don't care. I'm hungry and thirsty and tired. You said not to trust Algernon, and that turned out to be right."

"I never told you that."

"Yes, you did. In that big cavern."

"Oh," she says quietly.

"We always stay together," pleads Jake. "Are you staying with me?"

"I'm not," sighs Sandy. "I have to finish this. I wish I could explain. What about the real Algernon? Don't you want to save him?"

To Jake, that's not a fair question.

"I do. But…"

They stare at each other for a while. Peering down into the hole, Jake shakes his head. He wants to help, doesn't want to be upset with Sandy, but thoughts of home and the park fill his mind, blotting out all else. With a huff, he turns. One, two, three fateful steps.

Those steps make the difference. A terrific rumble shakes the ground. They hadn't felt any since leaving the valley, and this is a big one. Jake splays his legs wide apart to maintain balance, but that's all he can do. Looking back, he sees Sandy lose her footing and fall into the crack that she had been trying to get him to enter.

Then, worst of all, huge rocks splinter off from a nearby wall, plugging and covering that hole.

"Sandy!"

And the tremors stop.

Repeatedly scrambling over and around that pile of rubble, he searches desperately. But there's no way in. Digging is futile: his claws have no effect on the stone. There are some holes around the edge, but shallow, not allowing any sound or smell past that plug.

Barking her name, he waits, listens.

Again...

Nothing.

He's alone.

If he had stood with her, they'd be together. He would have been miserable again going downward, but at least he wouldn't be alone. Now, he has to hope that she rolled or skidded far enough to be out of the way when the rocks fell.

With a last look back, head and tail both drooping, he starts up the ramp.

Unfortunately, his path upward isn't the panacea he hoped it would be. Within minutes, after traveling through some twisting tunnels, he finds himself on another plateau. Orienting himself, he finds the edge and looks down. And there it is: clearly, the area he had left. A blurry shape is recognizable as that pile of fallen rock. A scan of the surroundings reveals nothing except a rocky plain stretching off into the distance, wall of rock on one side, cliff edge on the other. There are no other tunnels, hole, or cracks. He made the wrong choice for no good reason at all.

"Stupid Jake!"

His howl of anguish becomes frustration, then rage. More than anything he wishes he had a stick to chew to pieces. Or a rabbit to completely shred, like Sandy had done.

Sandy...

But she's lost and he can't do anything for her. It's hard to accept, but he forces himself to bury the grief that resurfaces. Thoughts of his lost friend trigger a cascade of memories, with the knot of emptiness in his gut influencing the direction they take.

Wait!

And an unprecedented inspiration strikes as those shared meals of rabbit and gerbil combine with the desperate need to get home.

I can do it!

Recalling the tower he had climbed with Ben in Thran, he imagines a spiraling path up, as far as it needs to be. But, rather than steps, he wants a ramp, like the one he came down at the beginning of this dream. And, at the tiptop, instead of a window looking out over the city, there's a way back to the waking world. As a final detail, one that he thinks Sandy would be proud of, he wants the thing to have been hidden for a long time and newly revealed by the recent quake.

Like he'd been taught, he pictures what he needs as a real thing, made of real stone. He knows it's here. Unlike the gerbils, though, it wouldn't come to him. He'd need to find it.

Knowing that it would make no sense for it to be in an open area, he heads back to the tunnel from which he emerged. The entrance would be somewhere along that wall, away from the edge. He begins to look for a pile of rocks. Near to that will be a crack or a hole. He can feel it.

Ever since arriving with Sandy onto the lower tier, Jake had detected the scent of a new type of creature. Traces had been scattered around, at times stronger than others, but it hadn't really registered in his tattered state. While on this search, that odor had grown steadily more intense. Exhausted, he doesn't even care to imagine what form the things may take or what their overall demeanor may be like.

However, the need to imagine isn't necessary: One of them is straight ahead, leaning against a pile of stones, facing away from him

My pile of stones, Jake thinks proudly.

And beside that rubble: a crack in the rock. The way up and out of this nightmare is right there!

Then it stands up, separating itself from the rock. Very much like an unclothed, hunched over man, but with canine traits in its face and body, it's neither. The thing doesn't leave, though. And, positioned next to the crack, there's no way to sneak past.

His exit so temptingly close, Jake hopes for the best and advances cautiously, tail awag.

Just be friendly.

The dog's movement is noticed instantly. But it seems to be stupefied by the sight, tilting its head and staring in the same manner that any dog would. Then it speaks, an outlandish jumble that sounds like the mewing of a cat. The basic words and concepts come through, though.

"Dog? Here?"

141

The tone of amused bewilderment is good enough for Jake. Hearing no hint of violence, he keeps moving forward and sniffs the thing. Like the vulture, an odor of decay is strong in its breath—and for good reason. Not far away on the ground is the partially eaten remains of what looks to be a human forearm, having been stripped of enough flesh for the bones to be visible. But beyond the obvious evidence, the distinct odor of death emanates from its pores, an excellent example of "You are what you eat."

Hesitantly, the thing touches him on the head, though it's less of a pat and more of a tactile confirmation that it is indeed seeing something in this place that it has never seen before.

With the bare minimum of niceties having been exchanged, Jake sees no need to wait any longer. He heads for the crack—and goes nowhere. A pair of hands grabs him by the hips and pulls him backward.

"No go there," it insists. And from within the mishmash of sounds, "New hole" and "Danger."

Danger?

Jake wants desperately to explain how this is his hole and that he had created it not long before because he really wants to wake up in his own home, and that it can't possibly be dangerous. But that requirement to act stupid and happy makes him hold his tongue.

Another attempt yields the same result, less gentle this time, hands grabbing him firmly by his haunches.

"No!" it scolds, then spins around to get in front of the dog.

From a young puppy, Linda had taught Jake that growling is rude. Ever bearing that in mind, he usually manages to suppress the urge when it strikes, especially when around people. But this weird thing isn't a person. And although protecting an unexpected dog from the unknown is commendable, he views the interference as irritating.

A growl forms, but dissipates, when the thing starts waving.

What?

"Here!" it calls out. "New hole!"

From the left, Jake hears the sound of something approaching. Then sees them. Two more. No, three.

All caution and etiquette are discarded.

"Get out of my way! It's my hole! I want to go home!"

Stunned comprehension of the words written into its face, the thing freezes—enough. Jake uses that small advantage to squeeze behind and in. Knocked off balance, falling, a hand snags his tail as he speeds by. But, by springing forward with all his might, it slips off!

He shoots up the ramp.

It's a long way, longer than he thought. Even longer than the tower stairs in Thran. And with every rest break he reflects on a design mistake.

First: no windows, no light. Having given no consideration to adding so much as a dull green glow, it's pitch-black. He's running blind again.

Second: no landings, not a single flat spot. Concerned with getting out as soon as possible, the route unwinds in one continuous, unbroken ribbon under his paws. The pauses he takes aren't exactly restful, as he needs to tense his muscles to prevent a slide backward.

Third, and maybe the worst: it's too big. Having been annoyed by the claustrophobic path up from the valley, and having grown accustomed to living with humans, he'd envisioned his exit as human-sized. And that means that it's perfectly large enough for those things to follow, large enough for them to explore this brand-new feature that has suddenly appeared in their world and chase down a talking dog.

And that's what they're doing.

With each stop, Jake hears their shuffling gait. How far away now? The sounds being funneled up to him, the distance is indeterminable, though louder every time.

Closer.

Getting caught by them and taken back down… Could there be anything worse?

Go.

He tries to get moving again, can't. Rebellious muscles, locked in place, refuse.

Go!

Not only the sounds of their feet reach his ears, but now, their panting breaths as well.

MOVE!

The threat behind growing louder, he forces one paw into motion, then another. His burning legs scream, but once cracking through that trap of inertia, the natural rhythm of walking takes over. Knowing he cannot let himself stop again under any circumstance, he concentrates on keeping a steady pace, hoping every second for the climb to end.

But it just keeps going.

Heart thudding, legs ready to fail, he pushes away despair and focuses…Finally, he smells it: the park. Earth and grass and flowers. The trees that all the dogs mark, and all of their individual scents. The people who accompany them. The pond with the water that is okay to swim in, but that has an odd taste. It's all there, in his mind, in his nose.

Where?!

The top of his head touches something.

What?

Shoving upward into something firm but flexible, bits of dirt break off and fall. It's a thick, woven mat of roots.

Underneath?

The aroma of moist soil is intoxicating.

I'm here!

Biting and tearing off chunks, he makes a dent, then a hole for his head. Getting a miraculous traction on the ramp, he pushes up frantically with his neck. The tip of his nose pokes through, filling his nostrils with marvelous odors. And even as he wonders if he can escape the hands that must be so close, ready to grab him, he falls—up!

Sucked or pulled, falling upward out of control, the wind swirls by faster and faster. Unable to see anything, his only thought is of the one thing that anchors his reality.

The park!

***

Jake cracked his eyes and inhaled. The smells of home were all around: in the air, on the floor. His favorite ball was within sight.

And SHE—another name bobbed in, then floated away—was asleep in the bed above. All was good.

Except…it wasn't.

As a tangle of dream memories fought for attention, he tried to straighten them out. The taste of sod was very fresh—and very unsettling. He wasn't allowed to dig holes, and was inside, so why…?

Escape.

Weird things had been chasing him up and up. He had needed to make a hole.

Sandy.

He had definitely been with Sandy. But something had happened to her.

Trouble!

And there had been a cat. The grey cat from the park. Though, it had ended up being not a cat.

Cat-not-cat… Bird-not-bird!

As the details flooded back, they clicked into place: the need for him to track down the bad thing from the park, taking the flight with the vulture, the smell of Zoogs, and the yummy taste of rabbits and gerbils. And he'd seen elephants!

But there was so much bad, as well. The misery inflicted on Ben, the new friend he'd made. Nearly endless climbing. The perils of crocodiles and snakes and scorpions. And Dholes! The terror and misery in that world far outweighed the excitement of seeing elephants. He had no desire to have that dream again. In fact, he would stay awake.

Drink.

Aside from being thirsty, his throat was sore. From what?

Sandy.

She had been trying to teach him to growl and howl a certain way. Was that a dream-memory or a real-memory?

Real.

That part had been real. In the park. Yesterday. And Sandy…was…still in the dream? Jake had been asleep, so she must have been, too.

Yes.

He was sure that she was home right now, asleep. It didn't matter that he had watched her fall into a hole that had been plugged up with rocks. He felt bad about fighting with her and leaving her, but that had been just a dream. The demands of thirst calling out again, he stood…

?!?!

The effort proved to be an incredible shock, his muscles protesting all the way. Once up, confusion locked his legs statue-stiff. He tested himself by inching forward a bit, then more. There was pain—or a less-than-ephemeral remembrance of pain—but nothing debilitating. More than anything it had been a staggering realization: His dream had been real!

That thought needed some digesting.

The trip down the stairs to the kitchen, normally a mindless task even in the middle of the night, took a long time. Strength and coordination were not lacking, but he deliberated over every paw placement.

One step at a time…

The water in his dish helped to ease the ache, but not the doubt. The coolness was as welcome as ever, but there was no comparison with the laps he'd taken from that first stream. Shaken by his trip with the vulture, that wondrous liquid had healed both his mind and body. Or had it?

Dream.

But if it had been a dream, why could he recall that pure taste so well? He lapped up some more, trying compare this experience with a memory that refused to fade. That detail was strange in itself. How long did dreams ever stick around? A sharply defined image might be there for a few minutes, especially if there was chasing involved. But it would inevitably blur into mush soon afterward.

Noticing some crumbs from dinner in the food dish, Jake licked them up. Good, but not as good as dream-rabbit. And dream-gerbil was better than anything SHE— *Linda!* —had ever given him. The crunch of tiny bones was so unique. And the taste of blood made his mouth water. He could have it again, if he fell back to sleep.

Not real!

Dream-gerbils might be a nice diversion, but he knew that such a feast would do nothing to sate the morning hunger. SHE/Linda would always provide solid food to fill his belly. Sandy may have taught him how to create animals in his head, but that's hardly a practical skill.

Sandy…

His small friend—his best friend—had berated him in that cavern for not thinking. Well, he was thinking now! He remembered the name Linda. And the scent of the thing they'd been tracking. And more. Lots more! He wasn't Stupid Jake any longer! Why did Sandy have to keep going?

Exasperated by her stubbornness, he pounced on a piece of rawhide, pretending that he had caught up with the false Algernon, the cause of his frustration. He imagined gnawing on the thing's skull. But the taste of cow was too familiar, quickly shattering the illusion. He pushed it away and sighed.

Dark.

It was sleeping time for people and dogs alike. Sunrise and breakfast were somewhere in the future. He knew he should go back to bed—though, while downstairs, emptying his bladder seemed to be a good idea. There was no urgency, but with the nights being a pleasant temperature at this time of year, the little door he used was unlocked.

He didn't make it to the yard. At the edge of the porch he looked down the stairs to find a grey cat sitting in his yard. Crouched down, legs bunched beneath, it looked directly up at Jake.

Algernon!

With those sour dreams lingering, he bared his teeth and narrowed his gaze. His *intruder* growl began to form, deep down. Something made him hold it in, however.

Wait.

Too many questions crowded into his brain at the same time, none with an easy answer.

Awake.

And, being awake, the harmless-looking Algernon at the bottom of the steps should be the real one. But the bad thing had been in both worlds, and in this one it's hard to look more harmless than a dead bird! Complicating the decision-making process further was the fact that his muscles ached due to a dream. It was as if he was straddling dream and waking, two paws in each.

Sniff.

There was only one way to be sure: He had to get a good, close up, nose-full of scent from whatever was sitting down there.

Relaxing, trying to convey an attitude of simple curiosity, he went down the few steps, a tricky procedure on wonky legs. With tentative tail wags, he approached. The cat remained where it was, eying him. When near, Jake repeatedly pulled in great lungfuls, searching for any trace of that odor that had been burned into his brain. All around, he went, nose to tail and back.

Algernon.

That interaction was apparently enough for the cat. He stood calmly, trotted across the yard, then leapt onto the garbage can and over the fence.

Following the trail in the grass, Jake reverified the traces of catness. After finding a good spot to mark, he was heading back into the house when a terrible din clawed apart the night. Similar to what he'd heard hours before, cats were screeching and hissing.

Signal?

He forced himself up the steps to the sleeping room. His legs more lively already, the achiness felt like the ordinary fatigue brought on by a typical day of running and playing. Finding a comfortable spot next to the bed, safe and warm, he laid down.

Tired.

He was ready to sleep again. But would he dream? Would he go down to that vast chamber? He wasn't sure he wanted to. But if he did, would Algernon meet him there again? Why had he shown up in the yard? And what about Sandy? He wouldn't be able to check on her until morning.

Dream…

***

The heavy mist is all around, once again.

Recognizing the dream for what it is, Jake debates what to do. He's curious about what had happened to Algernon and the bad thing, but Sandy is a far greater worry. Is this the same dream? If it is, does he need to rescue her from that cave-in? Can he?

So many unknowns can't be disregarded. He knows that he must at least find the priest and learn what he can.

He locates the wall, the entrance. He looks in.

Down.

Until recently, there had never been a particular attribute associated with the concept of *down*, good or bad. Now, there is, and it's not good. He sighs.

Sandy.

Jake takes the ramp down.

This time, Kaman-Thah is alone in the cavern. Jake keeps a steady, rapid pace as he covers the distance, the towering column of flame as impressive as on the previous visit. And having learned a lesson with the bizarre statues, there's no thought of even glancing at them.

"My friend," the priest greets him, "you…" He pauses, brow furrowed. "You did not pass me. How is it that you came to be here?"

"Well, we found the bad thing in the first temple in Kled after going up to the top of the tower in Thran. Ariadne helped with that, but I feel so sad about what happened to Ben! Ben helped me, and he was much nicer than the vulture. Algernon made sure the crocodile didn't eat us at the temple, but we got attacked by weasels that looked like they were there, but really weren't. Then we went into another temple and got chased by scorpions, then fell a long way, but we splashed into water. It was very dark and we had to watch out for giant Dholes. And Algernon turned out to be fake. We found out he was the bad thing! I was tired and wanted to quit, but Sandy wanted to keep after him. We argued, which I never like to do. When the ground shook so much that I could barely stand, she fell into a crack and a bunch of rocks fell on top. I couldn't do anything about that and wanted to get out, so I found a ramp that went up. It was a long climb, and weird dog people chased me. My legs still hurt— Oh, no they don't any more. Then I smelled the park and woke up."

The priest alternately smiles and frowns through the course of that winding summary.

"I believe I understand what you are saying," he says slowly, "but such a feat is nearly impossible."

"It was my legs that hurt," repeats Jake. "My feet are okay."

"I'm sorry, that's not what I meant. You said that you had a strong desire to awaken—"

"I really, really, really wanted to wake up."

"—and you found a way to do so that required much climbing."

"A lot!"

"But there is no connection to the waking world in that region."

"The dog people called it a new hole. And said it was dangerous. But it wasn't. That was my hole."

"I see." Kaman-Thah pauses, then nods before continuing. "Those were ghouls. From their perspective, it was dangerous. The short ramp you descended"—he points behind Jake—"and the much longer, seven hundred steps behind the flame that lead down to the Enchanted Wood. That is truly the only path available for dogs and cats and people. You did…find…something new."

"Find?" asks Algernon, hurrying over to join them.

"It is a humble word for a miracle of that magnitude," comments the priest. "The chance discovery of a heretofore unknown intersection of the dream and waking worlds within the realm of the ghouls, hidden for uncounted millennia, is an unthinkably unlikely event."

"Agreed," says the cat. "Create, then?"

"Far more unlikely. Unless… Could she have done it?"

"That must be the answer."

"Wait," says Jake. "You said she. Sandy. I came back here for Sandy. Is she here? Or down there?"

"I have not witnessed her ascend the stairs," replies the priest. "Ordinarily, that means that she has not returned from deeper dream. However, your presence here, now, introduces some skepticism. For the first time I cannot say for certain if she is or is not below."

"She is," responds Algernon quickly. "She is. And we will go find her, Jake."

"Okay. Good. How did you get away? She told me you were a prisoner."

The cat looks at the priest.

"At the— At the first temple in the jungles of Kled?" Kaman-Thah hesitantly asks.

"Yes. With the weasels."

"That wasn't much of a prison for a cat," says Algernon shakily. More confidently, he adds, "That thing didn't know who it was dealing with."

"Thing! Now you sound normal. You didn't sound like you when you started saying entity."

"And that was because…" begins the cat, but his voice fades.

"Because that wasn't truly you," supplies the priest. "The evil thing being pursued took your form."

Jake nods, then looks from one to the other. "Should we go?"

"We should," acknowledges the cat. "I need to help organize our forces and plan a strategy. Thran would be a good base of operations."

"But you did that," says Jake. "With Ariadne."

"Oh. I did, yes. But…"

"Are you feeling okay?" asks Jake. Concerned, he inhaled as stealthily as he could.

Smells like him, though.

"I am," says Algernon. "Just a little fur-filled. I feel that moving will clear my head."

When he heads to the top of the stairs, Jake says, "I thought you had to go down a different way."

"This time I'm allowed to walk with you."

Walk is hardly the word for their trip down the stairs. It's so rapid that Jake has to again wonder about the identity of the cat, recalling its nonstop pace between the two temples. But the odor of the bad thing isn't with him now, and after a while Algernon slows, visibly tired by the effort. Slows, but doesn't stop. He seems determined to push his legs to the limit.

At the bottom of the steps, Jake knows what to expect this time and handles the transition well. Taking a moment to sort through the array of aromas, it's actually a sound that catches his attention, something so brief that it hardly registers.

The sun rising, it seems to be fairly early in the morning. Algernon leads, heading east along the same path that they had taken days before. It's strange for Jake to smell his own scent laid out in a line. At home, that odor is everywhere in the house, yard, street, park. In this place, there's one easily trackable route from here to Kiran and Thran and through the jungles of Kled.

The alien aroma of Zoogs is also present, as it had been the first time through. But more intense. As if—

And there it goes again!

In these woods, with a spongy carpet of moss and fungus running right up to the edge of the well-worn trail, it's easy for the inhabitants here to tread lightly. Of the movements that Jake does hear, most are the scurrying of small animals. But some can only be classified as half-moves, as if a something consciously realizes that its passage is making too much noise and freezes. Algernon, always plowing on, doesn't seem to notice the minor oddities. Jake has counted at least four.

And, as they reach the bridge across the first stream, there's a fifth.

When they cross it, a sixth.

"Algernon," Jake calls out. "I think that—"

It's when the cat pauses that two brown rats with extra-long ears and rubbery, writhing whiskers dart out and block them from going forward. Two more rush out to prevent a retreat. Then a waterfall of activity occurs, the creatures materializing from behind trees and fallen branches. A ring forms, then closes in, surrounding them.

"Zoogs?" asks Jake.

The cat nods sullenly.

Questions from Algernon are ignored as the pair are pushed off the trail to the left and herded deep into the trees. Some of the Zoogs carry spears, but it's the sheer number that makes escape impossible. Every few steps, it seems as if more join the mob. And, despite lacking a need for stealth, they collectively make barely a sound.

A clearing emerges from behind overlapping trees, disguised so well as to be undetectable from more than a leap away. In their midst, grey and ragged, sits a single Zoog on a stump that has been carved into the general shape of a throne. As the troop approaches, they form lines on either side of the leader, between which Jake and Algernon are marched. Jake can see that its fur has many scarred patches, and that it is missing both the left eye and ear.

When they stop, the leader glares at the cat with its lone eye, then bares its teeth. The sharp fangs are nothing like those of a rodent. It chitters, a shrill sound befitting its appearance.

Algernon responds in the same language with what seems to be introductions, as Jake hears his name amid the chatter.

With much animated pointing, especially at his wounds, the leader goes on and on, sounding more accusatory the longer he speaks. He finally finishes.

"What did he say?" whispers Jake.

Algernon bows his head to the leader before explaining.

"He told me how much he dislikes cats, as his scars were due to the most recent war, prior to the latest treaty between the two races. He also dislikes the treaty, describing it as not even being fit for a ghoul to eat. But our current situation stems from the fact that...I...had made an arrangement for one intrusion through their lands, not two. Due to this second trip, he believes that I am a liar, and would have gladly had me killed had I been alone. He yet may."

"But I don't want you to be killed!"

"I don't either, but I don't know what to tell him."

For Jake, the solution is obvious.

"The truth," he says. "About the bad thing. How I found it, and how Sandy sent it here."

"I don't think—"

"I can do it. I'll tell you, and you speak in his language."

Before Algernon can object, Jake launches into his narrative.

But the leader doesn't want to hear any of it. Growling at the first utterance, he stands and motions a group of spear-carrying Zoogs forward. They close in on the pair, but Jake doesn't stop. And Algernon keeps translating for him.

A spear tip in the ribs is too much for Jake, though. "This is the TRUTH about the bad thing," he barks in outrage.

When Algernon echoes the outburst in the language of Zoogs with the same ferocity, one of the words seems to grab the attention of the leader. With a wave of his hand the weapons are retracted. Then he repeats that word back to Algernon.

The cat nods.

Still visibly upset, he snarls a command and sits back down.

"Start over, Jake. You have his interest."

With a wag, Jake begins again. Choppy at first, the dog and cat develop a rhythm that allows the story to flow with a minimum of pauses. The leader looks back and forth between the two as they speak, and, bit by bit, his anger transforms into concern.

When at last Jake goes silent, the scarred Zoog stares at him. "Truth?" he asks.

Hearing that one word makes Jake's head spin.

"This is the truth," he says. "You understand me?"

"Now, yes."

"Can we go and find Sandy and the bad thing?"

"Bad thing is very bad," he says gravely. "You eat bad thing?"

"Eat it?"

"Zoogs don't kill something unless they plan to eat it," explains Algernon, leaning in.

As far as Jake understands the plan, the cats are going to kill it. And possibly eat it, because he certainly can't fathom what goes on inside a cat's head. But, if a promise to eat the bad thing will allow them to continue, it seems like a reasonable thing.

"I eat it," declares Jake.

Having an intimate knowledge of the Wood, the Zoogs know the fastest route. A pair leads them almost straight north, far from any well-trodden path. To the casual eye, there is clearly no way through, and for a person there wouldn't be. But for creatures the size of Zoogs and dogs and cats, it's easy going—though it's necessary to know that a jog to the left *here*, then a right *there*, is better than vice-versa.

In the west, the top of an enormous mountain rises far above the treetops. Entering its foothills briefly, the extra elevation allows a glimpse of the River Oukranos to the east through some rare openings in the vegetation, its waters sparkling in the sun.

Not long after, they turn to the northeast. The forest through which they travel begins to look more normal to Jake: the layer of moss underpaw is replaced with fallen leaves and bare soil, the glowing fungus disappears, the trees thin out. At the edge of a field of wildflowers, the Zoogs get them going in the right direction and turn back.

As promised by their guides, an afternoon of steady travel takes them north of Kiran and brings them within sight of the walls of Thran. They had followed game trails through the wilder areas, and human-made roads when available. In those latter cases, they had hugged the edges in order to be able to duck into the brush when needed to avoid any possible trouble.

But no incidents had occurred over the course of those hours, despite the previous group of travelers they'd passed having included a large, black dog. Looking much like a Labrador Retriever that Jake knew from the park, it had hummed to itself while trotting along next to the cart. Stopping to take a scent, it had seemed to become aware of Jake and Algernon, but a word from the cart driver had been enough to get it moving again. And humming.

Having only stopped for drinks at convenient streams, and with their destination now visible, Algernon suggests taking a break to eat. Tired and hungry, Jake readily agrees. But he's in no mood to chase anything down. Already near a bush that looks to be the perfect home for a rabbit, he decides that is indeed the case. Within seconds he has his meal.

Algernon's eyes grow wide.

"How did you…?"

"Sandy taught me. Rabbit is good, but gerbils are better. Do you want some? There's a lot here."

"I would. Thank you."

"Don't you like rats or mice better?"

"I…do," says Algernon. "I do. But rabbit, when available, is fine."

With the two working together, it's an easy task to rip the carcass open and gorge themselves. The food and short break combine to reenergize Jake.

"I needed that," he says, licking his paws clean.

"Are you ready to get moving again?" asks the cat.

"We should go. Sitting too long will make me sleepy."

But he doesn't speak aloud the other reason he has for them to be on their way: a feeling of being watched. That's all it is, though: a suspicion. A hunch. Less than even the half-sounds that the Zoogs had made. There's nothing at all he can pick out definitively and say, "Look at that." The breeze also isn't helping matters, carrying no scents that might provide a clue to the identity of the watcher.

It's probably nothing.

160

With the sun sinking, the dynamics of the environment change, inviting nocturnal animals to start their activity. That different set of sounds prevents Jake from zeroing in on anything out of place. It's only when they enter a stretch blanketed with leaves and twigs that he manages to catch the subtle noises of purposeful stealth. The trees easily conceal whatever is watching them from his eyes, but not his nose. The wind finally carries a fresh, known scent.

"Algernon, there are cats here."

"Yes," comes a feline voice from ahead. "There are."

As the pair stop, one steps out from behind the trunk of a toppled tree. Then another. And one more on either side of them. They spread out and space themselves equally around the adventurers. The cats that Jake had encountered to this point had seemed to be perfectly fine—except for the fake Algernon, of course. These ones, though... Larger than average, with fur having grown back unevenly over scars, he can tell they are not housebroken.

"Who are you?" demands Algernon. "We are on a trail, and the mice are near!"

"*Mice*," he sneers. "I am Zachary. You, traitor to our race, can only be Algernon."

"Traitor?"

"You granted dogs entry here!"

"These are extraordinary circumstances," sputters Algernon. "I admit to making the suggestion, but the resolution—and the power—to do such a thing was not mine alone."

"I respect your honesty. The others will be dealt with, but the mistake that needs to be corrected began with you. The four of us bear witness to your confession. Four! More than required for

161

judgement. We all four also witnessed you dining with a dog. And if that is not disgusting enough in itself, you ate food that had been provided by *IT*."

The menace in his voice growing with every word, the final one had been stressed especially harshly. The vitriol seems to have an effect on the other three. They hiss in unison and shift forward, each gaining a few inches. Jake spins around to keep tabs on what's happening behind them.

"The Purists were eliminated centuries ago," spits Algernon.

"We can never be erased! The principle is rooted too deeply within us. It will *always* exist. There will always be those of us willing to fight for our world."

"This is not *our* world! It was meant to be shared. With humans and—"

"Humans! What have humans ever done for us? They're hardly better than dogs!"

There's an ear-splitting screech!

As if from thin air, three more cats bound in. As Algernon hurtles forward to take on Zachary, the newcomers match up with the originals. Four tornadoes form and spin. Tufts of fur fly. Blood begins to seep.

Unsure of what to do, Jake stays out of the way. Mainly he watches Algernon, trying to figure out how he might help. But he and Zachary are rolling and shifting positions so fluidly that he's afraid to put his nose in and bite the wrong one.

Two cries ring out at the same time, above the noise of the melee. One of the scarred originals is down, as well as one of the newcomers. However, before Jake can react the two winners zoom toward each other.

Just in time, he turns his attention back to Algernon: Zachary has pinned his friend and is getting ready to deliver a killing bite!

With a half-leap, Jake is there, clamping down on Zachary's left shoulder. Adrenaline fueling the attack, his teeth pierce skin and muscle then slip between the bones at a fatal angle, dislocating the limb. A yowl from the cat barely registers.

With that leg firmly in his jaws, Jake whips his head. Flesh tears but holds as the cat is jerked off of Algernon, and his wailing ends when head rudely meets ground. That front leg jutting out at an unnatural angle, blood spurts from the mangled joint a bright, bright red.

"YOU!" groans the cat, that single word coated in an acidic hatred. He tries to get up, but fails, legs twitching.

In his young life, Jake had never been in a real skirmish with either a dog or cat. There had only ever been minor, noisy squabbles. Mesmerized by Zachary's last breaths, this is far from minor. But worse than the guilt of killing is his inability to come to terms with the animosity that had driven the attack. His understanding of cats woefully inadequate to begin with, he stares down at the broken remains and searches for a reason for the bitterness he heard.

And searches.

And searches.

Dimly, he hears the sound of death twice more.

There is no answer to be found.

"…"

"…"

"Jake."

At last, the voice registers, pulling Jake from his funk. He looks up to see Algernon, fur matted with blood, but alive.

"You shouldn't have done that," sighs the cat.

"I didn't mean to," whimpers Jake, "but I had to save you."

"It would have been better to let him kill me."

"No! Why are you saying that?"

Algernon opens his mouth, then closes it and shakes his head. His eyes glaze.

"I am Penelope," announces one of the survivors. Pure black except for spots of white on her paws, she doesn't appear to have picked up a single scratch. "And this is Jeremy," she says, indicating the orange and white feline alongside her. "Our third, Andreas, fell to the vermin. But, among us, there are three witnesses to the act." She looks directly at Algernon, pauses, then says, "By law, as an outsider among us, you are required to initiate the proceedings."

With her statement, Algernon perks up. His brow furrowed, he pauses to look around at the carnage.

"I claim the exemption of deferred judgement."

Jeremy unleashes a guttural curse.

"That is your right," he seethes.

"Defer to whom?" asks Penelope calmly.

"It is not necessary to utter her name." Glancing at Jake, he adds, "Nor appropriate."

Her?

All three cats dip their heads. When they raise them again, Jake can feel that the tension is gone. Or, at least greatly lessened.

"Did you come from Ariadne?" asks Algernon.

"We did," replies Jeremy. "She suspected the Purists would reveal themselves."

"Then you know why Jake is here, and how important he is."

Jaw clenched, Jeremy flares his nose.

"We were not offered much in the way of explanation," says Penelope.

"Explaining now would waste precious time. We must get to Thran."

"There is no need to go to the city."

"Ariadne is near?"

"Near enough, but we must go. Another attack is possible. It would be best to rendezvous with her before nightfall."

Alternating periods of slinking and sprinting through the tame landscape around Thran brings the group to an encampment north of the city. Dozens of cats preparing to bed down for the night are suddenly on high alert with their presence, but a password from Jeremy allows them entry. They meet Ariadne at the center of the troop.

"It was as you suspected," Penelope tells her. "Zachary's grumblings were more than just words. He revealed himself as a Purist and led three others to ambush Algernon and Jake. They have been dealt with, though Andreas was lost."

"That is a shame," laments Ariadne. "He was young. And his death leaves our total at twenty-eight, an ill omen. Is there anything else to report?"

"Yes. And more than an ill omen, unfortunately. There has been a complication." She pauses before muttering, "Jake engaged in the battle and broke the prime law while defending Algernon."

Ariadne blinks, then hisses a curse. "A complication? That is possibly the understatement of all time! I have been charged with his—" Another curse. "And three witnesses?"

"Including Algernon, yes. But he has invoked a deferment."

"At least we have that," she sighs. "A temporary measure."

Wanting to relieve himself of some guilt, Jake opens his mouth to explain, but closes it when he sees Algernon shake his head. A second attempt to speak is met with a sharp rebuke of bared fangs.

But the cat composes himself and clears his throat.

"If I may?" Algernon asks Ariadne.

She nods.

"These are unique times. The threat is unprecedented. We all know that the transgression cannot be ignored, but, at the moment, we must do what needs to be done. And afterwards… We allow her wisdom to guide us."

"That is all we can do," agrees Ariadne. "Everyone, get some rest. Tomorrow will be…complicated.

At dawn, they eat. Jake is given only as much time, and breakfasts on the same thing, as the cats. When field mice stream in, he scoops one up. Not as bad as squirrel, the flavor reminds him of weeds. Or grass. And, able to chomp it down faster than the cats, he pounces on a straggler and downs it as well.

Then, they're off, heading north. With their numbers, there is no need to hide in shadows. They simply march.

Jake and Algernon start in the middle of a protective ring, but as they go, there are whispers from all around. And evil glances. The cats from along the sides move forward, ones from behind run past. During one such maneuver, a calico's claw finds Jake's hindquarters, drawing blood and a shocked yelp.

Eventually, the pair are left to bring up the rear.

The sun still hasn't peaked at noon when they arrive at a familiar-looking trail. A few sniffs from Jake are enough to confirm that it is the same one they had used on their trip west. No elephants are in sight, however.

When Ariadne calls for Jake and Algernon, the troop give them plenty of room.

"When we met in Thran," she begins, then stares at the blood in Jake's fur before continuing. "It was explained to me that the eastern temple would be the most likely place for the thing to go."

"We went there first," says Jake. "Then to the one in the west. On this trail."

"You're sure it was this one?"

"Yes. Our three smells are there. But they're not as strong as they should be."

"Jake woke up in the between time," interjects Algernon. "We both did."

"Ah, that was the reason for the delay," murmurs Ariadne. To Jake, she asks, "How old is the scent?"

He inhales deeply, then draws on his experiences in the park.

"Four days. Maybe more."

"Good," she says. "That's consistent. But all that tells us is that it didn't return to the eastern temple this way. Although there's no reason for it to be in the western one without its prize."

"Having located that," says Algernon, "it would travel this, the fastest route west."

167

"And so, we can conclude that it hasn't yet. That news is the—"

Some snickering catching her attention, Ariadne rushes at the calico that had slashed Jake and pounces on her. They roll and separate.

"I thought that mark on Jake looked like your handiwork, Esmerelda," she snarls. "You are reduced in rank. Step out of line one more time and I will have you banished!"

The chastised cat hangs her head.

"Listen up! I am commanding this troop! Together, we have a mission to deliver this dog to the eastern temple, and it shall not fail. It shall not!" All feline eyes look down as she scans the throng. "We are going there now. Jake will lead the way because he is the only one who can scent it. The only one! Do you understand that?"

As one, the cats meow their assent.

"It is possible that the thing may be heading our way. We may be forced to engage. You've all been briefed on its preferred tactics. I expect my orders to be followed. Again, do you all understand?"

Another chorus of meows.

"Jake, it is unlikely, but it may get past us. If you smell any trace of it that is more recent than four days old, you let us know immediately!"

"Yes, ma'am!"

"You all have ten minutes to eat and rest."

For a change, Jake leads. Head up, then down, he zigzags left or right at random intervals to try to get different nasal perspectives.

Fixed on a task like never before, an elephant would have had to step on him to be noticed. The hours pass, tense but uneventful.

Reaching the point where they have to leave the broad path, he guides them through the thick brush. Creeping as quietly as Zoogs, staying low, they get to the edge of the flagstone-covered courtyard and peer across the open space. There's no movement, nothing to hear, but there is one, very conspicuous change since the last visit: The crocodile is out of the water, at the far end of the bridge, blocking the way. Worst of all, with its jaws spread as far apart as they can go, the mesmerizing rows of cat-crunching and dog-gobbling teeth are revealed. There's only one way into the structure—through its open mouth.

"It wasn't like that before," says Jake, voice low. "The guardian stayed in the water except when we tried to go in. But Algernon knew the password."

When Ariadne looks at Algernon, he moves his head a small amount, an odd half-shake.

"It's of no matter," she says. "Before that problem is tackled, we need to determine if the thing is in the vicinity. Perhaps its attempt to enter brought the guardian to that position. Jake, I want you to check the entire perimeter."

"The *what*?"

"Go all the way around. Stay in the bushes, out of sight. Check for any odors that shouldn't be there. You've spent enough time in this jungle to judge what belongs here and what doesn't. Penelope, take two and accompany him."

The stealthy trip northward, along the western edge of the courtyard reveals nothing new. But within the greenery bordering the northern edge, the presence of a novel odor makes him stop. Pointing out a spot on the ground, he steps back.

"What's that?" he asks.

All three cats take a whiff and confer.

"Striped tree lizard," says Penelope. "They're rare, but known."

Adding that scent to his inventory, Jake finishes off the north edge and makes the turn at the next corner. It's during the check of the eastern side that he smells it. And strongly, too. The thing went by within the past day. Getting his nose as close to the court-yard as he can, then backtracking a short way into the jungle, he confirms its route.

The rest of the perimeter holds nothing else of interest other than the site along the southern edge where the thing had origi-nally entered the courtyard. As well as he and Algernon and Sandy.

Sandy.

Having been caught up in the chase, his thoughts turn to her for the first time since he related his waking and dreaming exploits to the Zoog leader.

It's here. She can't be far behind. Unless she's trapped. Or worse.

Doing his best to tamp down the worry, he holds onto the hope.

When he and the cats rejoin the troop, Ariadne has Penelope stay there with half of their numbers while she has Jake lead her to the fresh scent along the eastern boundary. Once in position, a signal call brings both sets onto the courtyard at the same time. Again, Jake leads, following the scent across the stones, but this time there are two cats on either side, ready to protect him. As expected, the trail goes directly to the bridge over the moat. As the groups converge, all eyes are on the reptile. But it never moves a muscle, or even blinks.

Jake steps onto the bridge for a sniff.

"I'm sure it went over," he reports. "But how do we get past the crocodile?"

"We do not," replies Ariadne. "*You* do."

Jake cannot believe his ears. Those two tiny words carry a suffocating weight.

"What?" asks Algernon.

"I was given several directives and sets of instructions for handling different scenarios. Protecting Jake and delivering him here were the prime ones. Having accomplished those, the mission becomes one of containment. The presence of the guardian on land implies that the thing remains a threat. Otherwise, it would have retreated back into the moat. Our target is not visible outside, so it must be within. If it does emerge, our job is to prevent it from escaping."

"And it will not leave the temple until it has found what it seeks," says Algernon. After a pause, he adds, "But once it does…"

"Precisely," she says. "Stopping the thing at that point would be a near impossible task."

"But you're asking Jake to do something equally impossible: both gaining entrance and confronting that creature alone."

"No. I ask nothing of him. What you describe is what he *should* do. He is the one who has somehow become linked to it. Despite that peculiar relationship, he has the right to choose his own course."

Eyes focus on Jake.

"Can I wait for Sandy?" he asks, hope welling. "She'll know what to do. She should be here soon."

"You may wait," replies Ariadne. "In the meantime, I may rely on my own wisdom and ponder whether your transgression has been deferred long enough."

"It is not appropriate to revisit that issue now!" claims Algernon.

"If I'm not mistaken," she quips, "it was you who stated so eloquently yesterday that these are unique times."

Glaring back, he says nothing.

"As leader of this troop, it is my right to make decisions at the time of my choosing! And it is entirely mine to make. No instructions were left for that eventuality and the need to shield him from harm no longer applies."

Algernon seems to calm, but then Jake notices his muscles tense.

He's g—

And sure enough, an explosion of grey fur attacks Ariadne. As her right paw flashes out defensively, Algernon jukes his head, but not enough. One claw snicks his nose, leaving an ugly scratch. The two engage fully then, rolling and tumbling. With Algernon not fully healed from his last scuffle and Ariadne plainly more skilled, it's no contest. He is soon pinned, and, blood lust filling her eyes, she truly looks as if she is going for the kill.

Though it's nearly a repeat of the previous day and Jake wants to help his friend again, he knows that he cannot.

"STOP!" he barks with as much force as he can muster.

Loud to begin with, the stone of the courtyard amplifies the sound. Ariadne flinches, stares at Jake, and blinks. Eyes clear of the madness that had gripped her, she hops off of Algernon.

"I'm going!" announces Jake. Looking at the cats arrayed around him, he adds, "Sandy was right. You can't—" Gaze falling on the battered Algernon, he manages to stop himself from speaking the full thought.

You can't trust any cat.

Is Algernon different? It's hard to say. Violence seems to be bred into them. Regimented, with so many laws, they not only go to war with Zoogs, but their factions fight amongst themselves. To the death! And it's okay if cat kills cat, but no one else is allowed... It's far too much effort to view the world through the crazy filter of a cat's eyes. Rather than even try, Jake prefers to face the obvious danger at the end of the bridge.

"If you see Sandy and I don't," he says to Algernon, "tell her I said she was right. She'll know what I mean."

When the cat nods, Jake turns and steps back onto the bridge. Through the fracas and his own outburst, the guardian had remained, statue-like, fixed in place. The need to show no fear—to either the cats or the crocodile—is foremost in his mind.

He advances.

Time slows.

Each step gives him an opportunity to scrutinize the monster blocking his way. The teeth are larger and sharper than he remembers. And there's actually not enough room between the bridge and the building to allow the thing to station itself squarely. With its head set at an angle, only the end of the lower jaw rests on the bridge.

173

Jump?

There's a chance he could clear it with a leap on the right side, but only a slight move of the head would be enough to get him. And, based on his first encounter, he knows it can respond that swiftly.

Those teeth!

Although Jake's heart races faster, calmness washes over him. *Fate* is a nebulous concept that had been unknown until now, but he views those teeth as something that he's *meant* to deal with. If they bite him in half, then they do. And if they don't, they don't. Either way, he's sure that his meeting with them will be over soon.

He stops in front of the creature. Despite a dry throat and lump of dread growing in his chest, that strange certainty lends him the power to speak.

"Err," he says, trying to repeat the word with the same emphasis that Algernon had used.

There's no reaction.

"Guardian, I need to go past you and into the temple. If you want to eat me, I'm not going to be able to stop you."

Again, nothing.

Taking a deep breath, Jake steps forward, through the open mouth.

Alive!

And not the least quiver from the crocodile.

A glance back at the cats across the moat gives him some amount of satisfaction, but he still needs to enter the building. At the entrance he does pause for a few seconds, then lifts a front paw...

At least I won't see it coming.

…and places it down past that line that separates inside from out.

In!

He doesn't look back.

Only moving far enough to the right to get out of the sight of the cats, he sits down. Eyes shut, the anxiety of the past minutes is panted away.

I made it!

Stupid cats!

Calm down.

Breathe.

Breathe.

Bit by bit, he feels more like his old self. More relaxed, but the need for caution front and center, he starts with a sniff. The scent he knows so well is very strong. There's no question the thing is here, but it's diffuse and directionless.

Everywhere.

Sometimes, though, he gets day-old odor, and sometimes he gets hours-old. As if it had passed by this spot multiple times.

Opening his eyes, the first feature he sees is the great gash that runs east-west in the roof. Recalling it from his last, brief visit, he can now tell from the clean edges that the puzzling design was deliberate. With sunlight pouring in, the place is infinitely more welcoming than the other temple. But one similarity between the two is the floor. The stone is smooth, providing minimal friction for his paws. And are there any cracks at all for his claws? None that he can find.

A glimpse to the left shows a similar layout, the interior separated into two pieces. The other has a hole in the roof, too.

May as well look here first.

The south wall is covered, floor to ceiling, in a tapestry of tiny pictures. Squiggles and lines mainly, but, here and there, simplified animals and human faces. The craftsmanship is exceptional, the figures in perfect alignment. Some of the patterns repeat, but nothing in Jake's store of knowledge allows him to be able to apply any kind of interpretation.

Bird. Eye. Man.

Tall statues, spanning from floor to roof, line the eastern and western walls. Made of a red stone, they look to be in the same style as the ones outside: people, but not with human heads.

The north wall is undeniably the most dramatic. Occupying the entire surface is a painting of a man with a bird's head battling a humongous snake. They're on a wooden boat, but instead of traveling on water, they float through a star-filled sky. The man's knife is stabbing into where the serpent's heart might be even as its coils are wrapped tightly around him. There's no clear indication of who might win, or if either would.

And, barely visible at the bottom right corner of the image is a doorway. A dark one. Clever shading of the surrounding painting fools the eyes into thinking that it's part of the boat.

Hmm.

He can head backward and explore the other large room first, but that would probably allow the cats to catch sight of him. He decides he'd rather stay hidden and keep them guessing at his actions—at least until Sandy arrives.

Forward.

The shadowy entrance contrasts forebodingly with the bright, open floor. Bit by bit, Jake regathers his courage as he sneaks forward. Stepping in, he pauses to let his eyes adjust. Left is the only direction, a hallway heading straight west. A dim glow at the end of the corridor promises a reprieve from the black unknown.

Go.

Hugging the left, he inches forward. Step by step, the light grows, resolving clearly into a doorway on the opposite wall.

Almost there.

But relief is short-lived. As he reaches that goal, a furious roar forces his tail down between his legs. Worse, a crash of stone on stone follows, reverberating through his bones. Stomping and muttering begin, but fade, suggesting that the thing is getting further away.

Peering around the corner, he spies a long room. A slit of a window in the eastern side, set close to the ceiling, allows light in. Nothing moves, whatever having been there now gone. Both of the long walls running east-west are lined with a series of slabs, all painted with a scene. Other than the rubble of broken stone at the far end, the floor is bare.

Safe?

Senses on high alert, Jake enters. As in the previous room, it's plain that great care had been taken with the decorations. All of those stones had been cut to the same size and mounted the same distance apart. All are intact except for the final one along the north wall, now shattered on the floor.

Keeping an ear out for noises, he tries to make sense of the panels. Each depicts the same snake and bird-headed man from the huge mural. Exactly what the first one means is a mystery to him, but after that the man's attacks upon the snake plainly grow progressively more violent. The broken one having landed with the artwork facing the floor, he can't see the ultimate injury suffered by the serpent.

The exit is in the northern wall, past the debris. As before, he can only turn left and take an equally long hallway west. But this time the light at the end is more defined. That gives him the confidence to proceed—until another roar makes him pause. With any and all noises echoing in the confined space, it's hard to determine if it came from ahead or behind. But he knows that being frozen in indecision is not a good thing.

Go!

Taking care to minimize the clicks of his nails on the stone, he keeps moving toward the light. At the end, a peek reveals a room as large as the first one, again with a long gash in the roof and statues lining the east and west walls. But this one has very little actual floor, a rectangular pit occupying most of it.

Slowly, Jake walks forward, eyes on the hole. A sand-covered bottom becomes visible. Then, a grey shape on that sand, huddled against the far wall. It's a familiar, grey, cat shape.

"I know you're not Algernon," Jake yells down into the hole. "The real one is outside. Who are you?"

Cat eyes look up at Jake, seemingly surprised by the voice, but then flare wider as they lock onto on something behind him.

Spinning around, he sees a man with the head and long neck of a snake. And the snake strikes at him! Jake avoids it, but backs too far. Having been near the lip, one paw goes over that edge. Then the other. With nothing for his claws to grip, he yelps and falls. Managing to stay vertical, rear paws touch the sand first. Hitting and rolling, he's down, frightened, but unhurt.

Standing at the top of the pit, the man-snake is dressed in only a knee-length black cloth and sandals. As the neck retracts, or shrinks, the dull, black eyes study the pair in the sand.

"That is Bast," says the snake mouth. "Only her voice can command the guardian in mid-attack as was done."

And the fake Algernon laughs! Or coughs. Weirdly, it sounds like a cat trying to bark.

"You are correct," begins the cat. "Only she can. But I am not Bast. And I do thank you for demonstrating that even all-powerful beings can be utterly stupid. I confess having needed some time to figure out the players in this drama, but you've been caught up in it for…oh… Has it been an eternity? Already? Time flies."

And, in a blink, Algernon becomes Sandy!

Jake bounds across the sand. Burying his nose in her fur, a great snuffle provides indisputable proof: It is Sandy!

"I underestimated her," Sandy barks upward. "I would have thought that, by now, YOU would have learned not to."

Glowering at the dogs, the man-snake unleashes a terrific hiss. "WHERE IS—"

Rudely shoved, it plummets into the pit. But, shedding all traces of humanity on the way down, an immense snake is what smashes into the sand.

Jake and Sandy retreat as far as they can, but really have nowhere to go. Tails to the wall, they bare their teeth.

"HERE! I am here!"

The voice is that of a woman with undertones of cat. Appropriately, that's what Jake sees when he raises his eyes from the writhing coils. A mix of the two, her arms and legs, feet and hands, are the only plainly human parts. Half-clothed in the same manner as the snake-man had been, her skirt, slit on either side, is instead white, hanging to her sandals. Small, fur-covered breasts bob lightly as she moves.

"Bast?" asks Sandy. "In your true form, finally?"

"My true form in this world. And in the sand: Apep, lord of chaos and illusion, in his." Smugly, she adds, "And lowly Apep never learns!"

Lightning fast, the snake lashes out, uncoiling with a tremendous energy at Bast. It nearly hits its target.

Nearly.

From nowhere, the crocodile appears, using its head to block the strike. After bashing into that massive jaw, Apep thuds back into the sand. Upon landing, however, it recovers quickly, charging Jake and Sandy. Its power and speed are no match for the dogs. They're caught and held.

"I do learn," insists the snake. "Guarantee me a safe passage, or these two will die." Mouth open, the exposed fangs hover over Jake.

"You are truly pitiful," sighs Bast. "If you do learn, you do not remember. This world is much different than the awake world. There are rules here."

Saying nothing, Apep switches to Sandy.

"You cannot kill them. If you could, you would have done so long before now."

"My poison acts slowly, giving hope of recovery before a cruel and agonizing death. But there is no cure. I can pierce one and wait for the death. Would you chance one?"

"I would," says Bast flatly. "Kill both, *if* you can."

Stunned by the words, Jake whines. He struggles, but can't move a muscle. Then he realizes that Apep could be holding him much, much tighter—could easily be squeezing the breath out of him, in fact.

The head of the snake bobs, back and forth, between the two dogs, as if trying to make up its mind which to attack. It comes close with feints, but never touches either.

"The smaller one granted you entrance here, and so you are indebted to her. And the larger one... He is not aware of the power he has over you. But I am. And you are."

"With the guardian at your side, I cannot strike you. But I hold these two. We are at an impasse."

"Not true," says Bast, shaking her head.

Kneeling down, she rubs the crocodile's throat. The mouth opens. Jake cannot believe what he sees, but she calmly sticks her arm in, all the way to the shoulder. Then the mouth clamps down, holding her in place, drawing blood! Moaning, she tries to free herself.

Apep acts with unimaginable speed, uncoiling from the dogs and shooting upwards, out of the pit.

But Bast reacts faster. With a tap of her free hand on the jaw, the mouth springs open. And when she extracts her arm, there's a golden object in her hand: a cross topped with a circle. With a whirl, she presents it boldly. The snake stiffens, then falls limply to the sand. Despite the blood on her shoulder, she shows no sign of pain.

"The key you so much desired was never inside this structure!" Her words are coated with gleeful triumph.

"That toy is not yours," snipes Apep. "You haven't the knowledge to use it properly."

"I know enough to hold you."

"Until you tire. And fall. I can see through you. I can see your ka. I have far, far more patience than you have energy."

The snake flexes suddenly, causing Bast to grip the object with both hands.

"I have enough," gasps Bast, "for Jake to complete the ritual."

"Me?" asks Jake. He's surprised to hear his name. "Do what?"

"The Overthrow," says Bast.

"NO!" yelps Sandy. "You can't ask Jake to do that!"

"There is no alternative. I can only bind Apep, and he spoke truly: not for long. Jake is the only one who can do what needs to be done."

"Wait," interjects Jake. "What am I supposed to do?"

Sandy claws at the sand and huffs. "You need to kill Apep," she murmurs, looking down.

"What?"

"You need to kill Apep," she repeats, more loudly. "There's a ritual. A set of actions."

Jake had been startled by what he thought he'd heard the first time. Now, he's aghast. The snake doesn't seem to be able to hurt him, but hopelessness gnaws at his insides. How can he possibly harm that gigantic thing at all? His teeth are good for rabbits and gerbils, but that scaly skin has to be far tougher than any rawhide he's ever chewed on.

"It makes sense now," sighs Sandy. "You took the first step while awake. When you peed on it."

"In the park?"

She nods. "And with you having begun the ceremony, you are the only one who can finish it."

"I can't!"

"You can! You have to!"

"Please, Jake," implores Bast. "Early in this journey, I admit to having doubts. But Oukranos saw the potential within you. He convinced me. Now, you have grown more than enough. You have the *strength* to do this."

Her voice, filled with encouragement, is a wonderful thing to hear, warming his heart. And the mention of Oukranos brings back a misty memory of that strange dream-within-a-dream in Kiran. But a look at the snake is enough to disperse the small amount of confidence that had begun to pool. And the eyes... When Jake makes the mistake of looking into those dull pits, it all goes.

"No," he sobs, shaking his head.

In the silence that follows, the protracted, hissing laughter of Apep freezes the panic-stricken dog.

"Yes, Jake. Be afraid. You are right to fear me. I am the chaos borne of night, but is your protectress any better? Do you honestly have faith in her? She has lied to you from the very start, first disguised as the grey cat, then as your friend. She is always hiding something from you. Do you know if she speaks the truth now?"

The question is an easy one. Unfortunately, the answer is also.

I...don't.

That awful realization transforms the stark clarity of terror into a haze of befuddlement. Jake's view of the world blurs. Before him are Apep and Bast. Really, though: a snake and a cat. Is one better than the other?

You can't trust any cat.

Bast stands firm, but her arms aren't as straight as they had been.

"Jake," she says, "y-you must trust me." She groans, her arms dipping briefly. "Please begin soon. Think. Use your mind to overcome—"

"Use your mind," mocks Apep. "I can at least respect the bravery of cats. I respect you, daughter of my enemy. But dogs? They're good for cowering in corners, only finding enough spine to slink out and lick up table scraps. You ask a dog to think? No dog thinks!"

No dog thinks.

Right then, the words do ring with a certain truth. The wheels and gears of Jake's mind are so clogged with webs of confusion and insecurity that it's difficult for him to make any sense of what's happening.

No dog thinks.

But those words get through.

No dog thinks.

Those words are a spark.

Stupid dog.

The spark becomes a flame.

Stupid!

The flame burns the webs.

I'm not stupid!

The conflagration spews out.

"NO!" he growls, frustrated fury encapsulated within that single syllable. Tearing across the sand, he bares his teeth and bites down on the snake. But it was as he originally suspected. Unable to pierce through that hide, they slide off.

"You cannot harm me, dog," scoffs Apep.

"What do I do?"

"Your rear, left paw!" shouts Sandy. "Step on him with it."

"That's all?"

"It's what's next. There's more."

Baffled by the simplicity of the act, Jake turns around and places his rear paw on the serpent. The entire length jerks slightly, as if shocked by a current.

"Now what?"

"We need a lance," says Sandy. "A pole with a blade on the end."

"Look beneath the sand," gasps Bast.

"Jake, dig!"

Sand flies as the pair search, but there's nothing.

"Hurry," begs Bast.

The painful urgency in her voice touches Jake to the core. He knows that feeling of wanting something so very badly. When he had been underground, that need to wake up, to escape, had driven him to find a way out. Whether he had created it or only discovered it didn't matter. What mattered was that he knew that wishes could be made real here—like with rabbits or gerbils or a ramp.

Lance...

Did he feel something other than sand where he fell into this pit? Maybe, maybe not. But, over there now, a small bit of wood is exposed. Little effort is needed to confirm.

"Sandy!"

Together, they uncover the end and pull. It emerges, roughly hewn but straight, the other end fitted with steel.

Letting go, Sandy explains, "Get a grip near the sharp end and stab Apep." She adds, "A small scratch is enough, but a big one is also good!"

The spear isn't heavy, but is unbalanced. The bare end drags in the sand as Jake approaches the snake. While trying to get a better grip, another glance into those baleful eyes makes him stop short. Trepidation takes hold and threatens his resolve. But only for a heartbeat.

You think I'm stupid? I'm not stupid!

Racing forward those last few paces, the blade sinks in, deeper than it needs to. Blood seeps out. There's a hiss from the snake—of anger or pain—and its eyes widen fearfully.

"Now we need rope," says Sandy. "To bind him."

Jake drops the spear. "Rope. Like a leash?" And even as he speaks, he knows that one is nearby, also under the sand. A thing that he has come to dislike for its restraint, at the same time it symbolizes the freedom of the park. Every day, after a short walk connected to it, he's able to run free in that grass-covered field surrounded by small thickets of trees around the edges—the perimeter, using the new word he's learned. Now, his leash will be put to a very good use.

It only takes a second to find, and the same as he'd imagined: black with gold writing, the same design repeated down its length.

The loop for a hand is at the one end, though the other purposely lacks the chunk of metal that clicks onto his collar. When he turns to face Sandy with it hanging from his mouth, he can see her beaming with pride, tail wagging enthusiastically.

"Good job, Jake! You need to wrap it around him. A little bit. It's symbolic. You just need the ends to cross…"

Sandy's voice fades into background noise. He already knows what he needs to do with the rope. Linda watches many shows with animals on the television. Aside from elephants and crocodiles, he has seen many more that he doesn't know how to label. Fascinated by any and all beasts, he had paid attention to those images, including how people capture them with nets and ropes. The snake being held still by Bast—though she looks to be struggling badly—will make the job easier, except for the fact that Jake has only one mouth and no hands. But he's confident he can make do.

Laying the leash down in a rough circle around the head, he grabs both ends in his mouth and drags it backwards, stepping to the side of the snake. But Apep refuses to cooperate, pressing its lower jaw into the sand. Knowing that a bite will have no effect, Jake tries to scratch with his claws. They also slide right off. Does it have no weaknesses?

And Jake sees that it does—two, in fact.

Thrusting a nail toward one eye is enough to trigger a reflexive response. With the head lifted, Jake draws back on the rope, getting it past the jaws and onto the neck/body. Jumping over the snake, he opens his mouth. The ends fall, crossing over each other.

Instantly, Apep stiffens, acting as if the rope has been wound tightly around the entire length of its body.

"I am bound," it wheezes. "You buy her precious minutes, but it will amount to NOTHING! And, when her strength runs out, I shall possess the key. I may not be able to harm you, but the legions at my command shall. My reign of darkness will begin—across all worlds!"

"Whatever he does and says, ignore him," Sandy cautions Jake. "He'll try anything at this point."

"What's next?" he asks. "It's pretty easy so far."

"You need to burn him," she replies, but he hears defeat in her voice.

"With FIRE?"

At home, the fireplace provides warmth in the winter, but at a safe distance. Jake has no desire to get his nose close to a flame.

Apep chokes out a laugh. "Find fire beneath the sand, dogs."

Jake looks up at Bast. Breathing normally, she seems to be less tense, but her attention is wholly on the snake. Jake was hoping for some guidance from her, but she can't help. This problem is completely beyond him. He knows that wood is needed to keep fires going but has no clue how to start one.

"Sandy, how do we do this?" he whimpers. "Sand doesn't burn."

His misery growing with each passing second, Sandy amazes him by doing an exultant spin. Her tiny tail dancing, she shoots over to the edge of the sand and digs.

"Jake, here!"

When he arrives, a smooth piece of wood is poking out of the hole she's made.

"Grab it."

Latching on, he can tell right away that it's more than a stick. The end hidden in the sand is weighed down with something. A gentle pull exposes a piece of glass, the wood of the handle wrapping smoothly around its edge.

"It's a lens," she explains. "And it's made from sand! We need to get into the sun."

Being later in the afternoon, only a small spot of direct sunlight makes its way through the opening in the roof, but there is enough, and the tail of Apep lies within that patch.

"Don't look down," says Sandy. "You won't be able to see what's happening, but I'll guide you. Pay attention to what I say. And when I do tell you to move, do it very slowly. A little at a time."

And Jake does exactly that. He can see Sandy and Apep, but it's plain that the lens-thing isn't anywhere near the snake. How can tilting his head forward and back, or moving it up and up and up, no, down have any effect? Frustrating seconds go by, becoming minutes, as he makes what seems to be the same corrections, over and over—

"There!" yells Sandy. "Hold it steady! Good!"

And he hears it first, a miniscule crackling sound. Then smells the unmistakable scent of burning flesh as a wisp of smoke rises.

"NOOOO!" The wail from Apep seems to hold more despair than anger or pain. "How?" it whispers.

"That's it," Sandy tells Jake. "You can put it down."

"What did I do?"

"That." It's a blackened spot, barely the width of a claw. "You beat a god with science."

"How much more is there?"

189

"The toughest part is over, but the worst is— You're going to need to—" She sighs. "You need one more tool."

Returning to the hole in which the lens had been, Sandy pushes the sand around. After a few moments she pulls something out. Dropping it next to Jake, the short metal blade pierces the sand. He knows what a knife is, but the handles are always in line with the blade. On this one, it's perpendicular.

"I had a katar at one point," she says. "Seeing you struggle with the magnifying glass reminded me. This is a push dagger. It'll be easier for you to use."

"To do what?"

"Jake... You're going to have to finish this, regardless of how bad it seems. I think it'll be better if you do what I say, when I say it. Don't think about it. Just do it. And remember that, at the end, the goodness that comes will far outweigh any badness you may feel."

"That doesn't help, Sandy."

"It's the best I can do right now. Bast can't last much longer. Grab the blade and go over to Apep's head."

Getting a good grip on the handle, Jake pulls it out of the sand and walks over.

"Jab the blade into his eyes. It doesn't matter which one is first."

Not expecting to hear that, he hesitates... and the eyes that he is supposed to poke out focus on him.

"Lowly creature," wheezes Apep. "If you can pull your tail away from your testicles and find an ounce of courage, you shall vanquish me. But know this: As I die here, so dies my inability to harm you. I have known death before and it has never truly stopped me. You have earned my eternal wrath. But even now I yet have the power to look inside you."

The threat had struck home with Jake, but that final boast only puzzles him. And as he wonders what might be inside to see, there's a groan from above and behind him.

Bast!

He needs to act, and does. Moving forward, he stabs into the right eye. There's a scream of agony, and dark red blood oozes. Cringing at the sight, Jake closes his own eyes. But when he opens them, it's to a scene far, far more horrific than any nightmare he's ever had. It's not Apep who is trussed, unmoving, with one empty, bloodied eye socket…

Linda!

It's *his* Linda. Hands and feet tied, she's bleeding. Suffering. And *he* did it. Jake is the cause of her pain! His belly is empty, but still it churns. The knife falls from his mouth…

Oww!

A pain in his leg brings Jake back. Somewhat. Bound and bloody, Linda lies there, on the sand. And Sandy stands next to her.

Oww!

She bit him! Again!

"Jake! It's not real! Apep is doing this. It only looks like Linda. The real one is home, asleep. You'll see her soon. I promise! Just finish this."

Her words make sense. They most definitely do. Moans from above also register, make him look up.

"Bast doesn't have much strength left," adds Sandy.

And Jake can tell. He can see her arms shaking. The desire to finish is there, within him, but shock holds him in its icy grip.

"The *real* Linda," pleads Sandy. "Do it for her. If she could only know how much you've learned, she would be so proud! Please, Jake."

The real Linda.

With a stiff nod, he grabs the haft of the knife in his mouth.

This is Apep-Linda.

And steps forward.

Not-real.

And stabs her left eye.

The cries of Apep-Linda become screams, nightmarish sounds so intense that they seem to make the world tremble.

Dimly, he hears Sandy say, "Now cut the tongue out."

Tongue.

At that point Jake disconnects. He knows that he is the one plunging the blade into her mouth and shaking his head back and forth. And he feels the metal knocking against teeth. And he hears a choking gargle. But at the same time, he refuses to believe that he's part of it.

And when a blood-covered chunk of pink flesh lands in the sand, he covers it up and pretends it's not there.

"Cut open the chest."

The blade is surprisingly sharp. Whether it cuts through real ribs, or imaginary ones, it does the job well.

"And find the heart."

The blade seems to move on its own—because, certainly, he's not the one moving it. The incision grows larger. He searches for something within the gory cavity that moves.

192

"There," says Sandy. "Now eat it."

Ba-dump.

With those words, delusion dissolves. There is no escape from the moist reality of a beating heart, inches away.

Ba-dump.

He had told the Zoog he would eat the bad thing.

Ba-dump.

He recalls a summer picnic in the park.

Ba-dump.

The delicious taste of an uncooked steak that had fallen to the ground.

Ba-dump.

Would it be the same?

Ba-dump.

He sticks his snout in, chomps down. Blood squirts. Closing his eyes, he yanks.

And falls backward.

And chews.

And swallows.

But that lump never reaches his stomach. He feels it grow smaller, dissolving into nothing.

Which is a shame, because it *had* tasted like steak.

How much time passes while Jake stares at the pristine sand, now empty of snake, empty of blood? It's hard to say for sure, but not much. Light and sky are visible through the roof, though the sun has moved on. Sandy sits nearby, waiting. Bast and the crocodile are on the edge above, both also quiet and unmoving.

The spear, rope, lens, and knife all lie in the sand, but that's the limit of the proof that any of it had occurred. The taste of blood and meat in his mouth isn't a taste, but a memory of one—and fuzzy, at that. His head hurts as he tries to fix on the details. It doesn't seem to be worth the effort.

Just forget it.

"I guess we did it," he says.

Bast stands, jumps down into the sand, landing as softly as a cat.

"*You* did it, Jake" she says. "You."

When she beckons the dogs over, Sandy runs to meet her. Jake starts, but stops and looks back. Some aspect of the leash calls out to him. Even more than the bravery it took to stab the Apep-Linda in the eye, it symbolizes a breakthrough for him. He trots back to grab it and is glad of the measure of comfort it provides.

When he returns to Bast, she scoops up the dogs. With a powerful leap, they leave the sand behind.

Apprehensive is a mouthful of a word for Jake, but that's how he feels as they exit the temple. A flash of boldness had given him the idea, and Bast did not object. Her whiskers twitching at the suggestion when it had been made, she had actually appeared to laugh. At least, to Jake, still learning about cats, it looked as if she had.

With Bast striding out, holding the golden key—an *ankh*, Jake had learned—the crocodile lumbers beside her. And atop its head and shoulders sit Sandy and Jake. There's a flurry of activity as the cats run forward to get a look before seating themselves in an arc in the courtyard.

At the edge of the moat, the small procession stops and the dogs hop off their ride. A gesture from Bast causes the guardian to open its mouth, whereupon she kneels down and places the ankh far back into its throat. Jake holds his breath, fearing a chomp, but she removes her arm without incident and directs the scaly monstrosity into its watery den. The bridge being large enough to accommodate all three, they walk together. Bast seems to allow Sandy's small strides to dictate the pace, taking care to not get ahead of the dogs. Once on the other side, she stops them.

"The thing has been defeated!" announces Bast to the assemblage. "As suspected, it was Apep, lord of chaos. The worlds of both dream and waking are now safe. Jake was entrusted with unenviable tasks and performed admirably."

Proud, happy, Jake wags. But there is not a glimmer of relief or satisfaction to be seen among the stony-faced felines. His tail stops. He drops his rope.

What's wrong?

Algernon says nothing, but there's muttering from the rest of the troop. Ariadne listens, then quiets them down.

"But the dogs did send it here," she says. "This crisis was initiated by them."

"It was," agrees Bast. "And that was not an ideal action to take." She pauses to look many of the cats in the eyes. "However, the amount of damage and bloodshed that could have been inflicted upon the waking world is unthinkable. Banishment here removed that immediate threat. The game of illusion and deception that we played required patience. And Apep is not known for his patience."

Ariadne nods, then looks at the rest of the cats. When none speak up, she asks, "And what of the transgression?"

"What of it?" snaps Bast.

Ariadne recoils, but finds her voice.

"With your presence, High One, the time allotted for deferment, as requested by Algernon, is ended. A judgement is needed."

"No."

Stunned silence turns into murmurs, many confused. Some are angry.

"I beg your pardon," says Ariadne. "Can you please explain?"

"The minimum requirement of three witnesses is not met," says Bast. "I was masquerading as Penelope at the time of the alleged transgression. Although I act in the interests of cats, it is a fact that I am not one. The proper forms cannot be observed. My testimony cannot be included."

It seems to Jake as if about half of the cats hiss their indignation. Bast's eyes narrow at the reaction and land on Jeremy and Esmerelda.

"Only minutes ago," she yowls, "I stated quite plainly that this dog saved two worlds! And yet you insist on mindlessly adhering to the letter of the law?"

"The law exists for a reason!" argues Jeremy.

Scowling at him, Ariadne raises a paw and unsheathes her claws.

"And according to the Council of Elizabeth," he continues, "there is precedent for a majority vote to settle the case in lieu of formal proceedings."

Bast sighs, a sound of sadness so deep that Jake feels it in his own heart.

"Divide yourselves, then," she commands, pointing. "Those in favor of the strict application of the law, and those who see the wisdom in granting an exemption."

When the cats begin milling around, Sandy nudges Jake.

"Get ready to fight," she warns him quietly. "Or run. South, across the courtyard and through the jungle will get us to the river. We can swim to the other side."

The cats having separated themselves, Jake sees two groups of roughly equal size. It gets tough for him counting past four, so he stops. Sandy relaxes, slightly.

"What are the numbers, Ariadne?" asks Bast.

"Thirteen for, thirteen against. I am uncommitted."

"The oath of protection I swore of you no longer applies," Bast explains. "You are free to choose."

"Of that I am aware. You were very specific."

"While in the guise of Penelope, I witnessed you nearly kill Algernon over the right to prematurely make this decision. It is now rightfully yours."

In the group on the right, Jake can see Algernon tensing.

"I have lived my entire life by our laws," begins Ariadne. "It had been difficult to imagine a scenario where a violation of the prime law could be ignored. Now, for the first time, a perfect instance has been presented. I vote for the exemption."

That sounds like good news to Jake, and Sandy's happy yip confirms it.

"Therefore," continues Ariadne, "as leader of this troop, I declare th—"

A screech from Jeremy stops her words. As he advances toward Ariadne, the rest of the cats back away, leaving those two within a circle. There is hardly a pause as they collide in a flurry of claws and fangs.

"What's happening?" Jake asks Sandy as the first clumps of fur fly.

"He challenges for leadership," explains Bast, kneeling down. "Such a challenge, when made, must be accepted."

"But why?"

"Shh. This must play out to the finish, and I may not interfere."

The two combatants, equally fierce, attack and defend. Not a sound comes from the audience, not even when Jeremy has his throat raked by Ariadne, or when he succeeds in slashing through one of her eyes. That wound is too unnerving for Jake, and he turns away. It's shortly afterward when the sounds of battle end, replaced by the gasps of a single cat trying to catch its breath. And when he looks, it is Jeremy who stands victorious.

"By right, I am now leader," he proclaims. "Ariadne was given a chance to make the correct choice. She failed to do so."

"There is no majority in thirteen and thirteen," shouts Algernon. "You may not declare anything!"

"That was his goal," says Bast, standing. "It is a fact that we all witnessed Ariadne not finishing her decree. With the matter unresolved, Ariadne's protection as leader does not come into play."

As Jeremy sits high and smug, Algernon shrinks.

"However," begins Bast, stepping forward. "MY protection applies! To Jake, and Sandy, and Algernon. For the remainder of their trip through dream to waking, they shall NOT be harmed. Is that understood?"

Twenty-six cats meow as one. Some louder, some softer, but all.

"Jeremy. You have split this troop in half. The entire issue might have been buried under oaths of secrecy by Ariadne. We'll never know. But now, word will spread. More division will ensue. You would pit brother against sister to prove a point?"

"High One, it is more than that. The law is unambiguous. This trouble began with me blindly obeying orders to protect a dog, dispatching a Purist. I now find myself wondering if their creed is so wrong."

Jake can see Bast's jaw clench momentarily.

"It is not my job to herd cats," she says. "Govern yourselves as you see fit. I will ever be available to dispense help, or wisdom, when called upon."

Led by Bast, Algernon, Sandy, and Jake follow. No words are exchanged as they tramp back through the jungle, heading west. Once on the elephant trail, Bast has Algernon wrap his front paws around her neck and hold tight, then lifts Jake and Sandy in each arm. Starting at a slow pace, she develops a phenomenal speed. Only minutes are needed to cover the same distance traveled by the ill-fated troop of twenty-eight at the start of the day. They arrive at the camp site north of Thran as the sun dips under the horizon.

One segment of guard duty apiece sees them through the night. During Jake's shift, his imagination is on high alert. Every rustle in the brush or grass is a vengeance-filled snake. But his rope lends him the confidence to handle the next one that may come along.

In the morning, Bast gets them to the edge of the Zoog territory. Before she leaves, Jake and Sandy both give her licks of appreciation, with Algernon watching the complete lack of decorum in horror. But Basts's whiskers twitch while the dogs' tails wag.

A pair of Zoogs show up soon afterward. Then two more. And two more. The undergrowth is alive with torrents of furry, brown creatures, some running ahead, but most parading behind. They make no effort to hide themselves.

"Those are the Zoogs?" asks Sandy, seeing them for the first time.

Algernon nods.

"There are so many," she whispers. "Is this good?"

This time it's Algernon's whiskers that twitch.

"Not too long ago, I would have said no. But now, yes. It is good."

"Why are they all around us?" asks Jake.

"They're anticipating a good story," replies the cat. "And Jake, you will tell them. But make no mention of Ariadne, Zachary, Jeremy, that whole affair. The politics of cats are our own business. No one else's."

Straight to the leader they go, the horde gathered round him. Without any preamble, his first words are a question to Jake.

"You eat it?"

There's a tense silence as all wait for the reply.

"I eat it."

A smile forms on the scarred face. When he points at Jake and shouts, a chorus of Zoogian cheers erupt. A motion of his hand quiets all.

"Say how. Say all."

And Jake does. Carefully editing the tale to exclude details that may cast cats in a bad light, and with Algernon translating, the story of his triumph over the snake is related. At the very end, as another wave of cheering dies down, he looks at the leash. As much as he wants to keep his trophy, he realizes that he can't take it back to the waking world. Scooping it up in his mouth, he drops it in front of the leader.

"You can have this," says Jake. "You might need it to tie up a monster."

Slowly, the Zoog reaches down and picks it up. Despite it being so alien, the look of awe and gratitude is easy to read. With a command, eight Zoogs approach. One by one, they closely examine Algernon, Sandy, and Jake. All scatter into the surrounding Wood.

"They go," says the leader, indicating the eight. "They say to all: I protect you and you and you. Always!"

"Thank you," says Sandy, stepping forward and bowing. "We may need it."

With an army of Zoogs surrounding them, the trip back to the cave with the stairs leading upward is free of incident. If anything, it's amusing to Jake, with small groups peeling off and melting into the thick woods, only to be replaced by others that suddenly appear, as if by magic. They all want a glimpse of the hero, explains Algernon.

The trek up the steps is more pleasant than his last mad dash up through his tower, but still an effort, especially for Sandy. There's no need to hurry, though. They take their time, giving her plenty of opportunities to rest.

In the cavern, Kaman-Thah's greeting is as warm as ever, perhaps more so. The man beaming with delight, Jake gets the impression that, lacking the cat, he would hug the dogs in a very joyous—though exceedingly unpriestly—manner. But Algernon's presence seems to inhibit him.

Jake begins his story enthusiastically, but the cat takes control of the narrative, relating an abridged version of the incidents overlayed with outright fabrications. Algernon's injuries, for example, are attributed to a bear attack. Through it, the priest seems to wants to ask questions, but they go unvoiced. And as the sterilized tale unfolds, the man simply listens to what is purportedly the truth, though Jake does notice him pay increasing attention to his tail. Only at the end does the unfailingly honest dog become aware that he had been giving hints through his own, unconscious reactions to the words: a wag for truth, motionless for a lie. That, at least provides him some measure of satisfaction, but their final goodbyes to Kaman-Thah are uncomfortable.

Part of the way down the statue-lined hall, however, Sandy asks Jake and Algernon to wait as she returns to the priest. Their interaction is brief, the man nodding twice, and she runs back, offering no explanation.

At the far end of the cavern, the three look at each other. Without a word, Algernon moves off to the left and slinks into a cat-sized hole. Then Jake and Sandy ascend their ramp into the mist, and from there…

***

Jake woke, the reassuring odors of home hitting harder than possibly ever before. Blurry, terror-filled memories lurked in the shadows of the sleeping room, memories of snakes and cats and blood. But there were no cats in the room, much less snakes. The images sharpened and he knew that he had vanquished not only a snake, but a terrible entity named Apep. He remembered the joy in the face of the priest, and the sworn protection of the Zoogs, and the nonsensical and sickening hatred of the cats for dogs. And the miles and miles he had walked. And the sweet taste of gerbils. And the anguish of poor Ben. He could recall the whole thing.

And arching over everything there was…pride.

Safe.

He knew he was. And Linda was. And Sandy.

All safe.

The window dark, it seemed as if it would be a while until dawn colored the sky. It was time to sleep.

When Jake next awoke, the sun had risen. Outside in the yard, its rays warmed his fur. He stood there and mulled over the events of the long night. The familiarity of his own small yard was certainly satisfying, but the excitement of an unknown adventure was, too. Then he realized he could have both day and night worlds and wondered what Sandy thought about going back.

After breakfast, the trip to the park was especially welcome. It seemed as if he hadn't been there in days and days. He ran with Sandy and Butch, as well as a new puppy named Rusty. Oh, Rusty was so young and clumsy, with so much to learn. Jake decided he would teach Rusty to stay away from BAD things. And maybe catch rabbits. And, when Rusty was a little bit older, Jake would tell him about the dream world, and how to get there.

So tired.

But playing with Butch was hard work. Exhausted, he and Sandy headed over to the shade for a lie-down. And right before his eyes closed, he caught sight of a grey cat beneath a nearby bush, a patch of white on its chest.

Algernon?

The cat meowed.

So soothing.

And again

Just a nap.

Then a third time...

Acknowledgements

I would like to thank Swati for providing colorful details that I would not have been able to discover on my own.

You, too, can enjoy her insights at:

onethingleadstoanother470998289.wordpress.com

Born and raised in Pittsburgh, PA, Daniel Reiner was formed not of clay, but of peanut butter. And it wasn't the Holy Spirit that gave him life, but an unhealthy does of Warner Brothers cartoons. Spending his formative years at Carnegie Mellon University, it was there he discovered the world of H.P. Lovecraft in the old Del Rey paperbacks. Later, with a burst of creativity, he eventually became comfortable enough in that world to carve out his own niche, and populate it with memorable characters.

A lover of dogs of all shapes and sizes, his readers can be assured that any dog appearing in his writings will never be killed by a monster, human, or otherwise.